"My name is Alex."

"Your name is Alexei Nicholaievich Varenhoff, so christened in the Rovenian Orthodox Church. Your people know you as Prince Alexei."

"Look, this isn't real. They're not my people. I'm not Rovenian. I was born here."

His eyes sweep over me and a trace of emotion flickers across his features. "You are not English, Highness."

"I'm not Rovenian, either!"

MELISSA WYATT

RAISING
THE
GRIFFIN

LAUREL-LEAF
BOOKS

Published by
Dell Laurel-Leaf
an imprint of
Random House Children's Books
a division of Random House, Inc.
New York

Visit us on the Web! www.randomhouse.com/teens

Educators and librarians, for a variety of teaching tools, visit us at www.randomhouse.com/teachers

ISBN: 0-440-23821-8

Reprinted by arrangement with Wendy Lamb Books

Printed in the United States of America

July 2005

10 9 8 7 6 5 4 3 2 1

OPM

�֎

For Andy, Ned and Will, my princes

�֎

ACKNOWLEDGMENTS

For generous help and support, many thanks to Kristina Cliff-Evans, Joanne Nicoll and Elizabeth Patera for getting me started; Cathy Atkins, Laurie Calkhoven, Lisa Firke, Alex Flinn, Marjetta Geerling, Amy Butler Greenfield (and David), Shirley Harazin, Jennifer Page, Becky Rector, Shelley Sykes, Laura Weiss, Nancy Werlin, Linda Zinnen and the members of YAWRITER for keeping me going. Thank you to Alison Root for your insight and enthusiasm.

Very special thanks to Amanda Jenkins for first helping me see the forest *and* the trees. And to Wendy Lamb, for understanding and loving Alexei almost as much as I do.

A grateful thank-you for technical assistance to Chrissie DiZuzio, Debra Duer, Ken Kriefski, Deborah Mills, Becky Wright and Edward Wyatt.

THE VARENHOFF DYNASTY

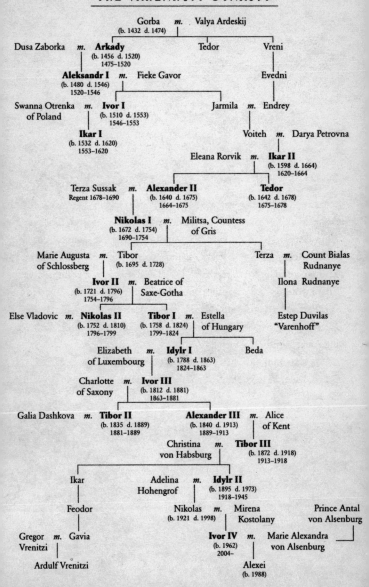

Gorba (b. 1432 d. 1474) m. Valya Ardeskij

Dusa Zaborka m. **Arkady** (b. 1456 d. 1520) 1475–1520

Tedor

Vreni

Aleksandr I (b. 1480 d. 1546) 1520–1546 m. Fieke Gavor

Evedni

Swanna Otrenka of Poland m. **Ivor I** (b. 1510 d. 1553) 1546–1553

Jarmila m. Endrey

Ikar I (b. 1532 d. 1620) 1553–1620

Voiteh m. Darya Petrovna

Eleana Rorvik m. **Ikar II** (b. 1598 d. 1664) 1620–1664

Terza Sussak Regent 1678–1690 m. **Alexander II** (b. 1640 d. 1675) 1664–1675

Tedor (b. 1642 d. 1678) 1675–1678

Nikolas I (b. 1672 d. 1754) 1690–1754 m. Militsa, Countess of Gris

Marie Augusta of Schlossberg m. Tibor (b. 1695 d. 1728)

Terza m. Count Bialas Rudnanye

Ilona Rudnanye

Ivor II (b. 1721 d. 1796) 1754–1796 m. Beatrice of Saxe-Gotha

Else Vladovic m. **Nikolas II** (b. 1752 d. 1810) 1796–1799

Tibor I (b. 1758 d. 1824) 1799–1824 m. Estella of Hungary

Estep Duvilas "Varenhoff"

Elizabeth of Luxembourg m. **Idylr I** (b. 1788 d. 1863) 1824–1863

Beda

Charlotte of Saxony m. **Ivor III** (b. 1812 d. 1881) 1863–1881

Galia Dashkova m. **Tibor II** (b. 1835 d. 1889) 1881–1889

Alexander III (b. 1840 d. 1913) 1889–1913 m. Alice of Kent

Christina von Habsburg m. **Tibor III** (b. 1872 d. 1918) 1913–1918

Ikar

Adelina Hohengrof m. **Idylr II** (b. 1895 d. 1973) 1918–1945

Feodor

Nikolas (b. 1921 d. 1998) m. Mirena Kostolany

Prince Antal von Alsenburg

Gregor Vrenitzi m. Gavia

Ivor IV (b. 1962) 2004– m. Marie Alexandra von Alsenburg

Ardulf Vrenitzi

Alexei (b. 1988)

1

I crouch low on Drummer's neck, leaning into his rocking gallop. He's mad, tearing across the field at top speed. I can't hold him and I don't try. We pass Herald and overtake Wilkinson, who swears at us, and slow as we go into the wood. Drummer strains up the hill, making it a little easier to pull him up and wait for the others.

"What's our excuse this time?" I say, once we're all gathered on the top of the hill. Below us, the open hillside slopes down to the school, where we were due back from a cross-country ride an hour ago.

"We got lost," Herald says with a shrug.

"Third week in a row?" I ask.

"Collectively, we have a very bad sense of direction." Herald bends over and pulls a thin flask out of his boot.

"Except where pubs are concerned," I say.

Herald opens the flask and takes a swig.

"Tell 'em the truth," Wilkinson says. "Varenhoff here wanted to see that blond barmaid with the big tits again."

"And then was too much of a poncey twit to chat her up." Herald passes the flask to Wilkinson.

"I talked to her!"

"Varenhoff," Herald says, "'Can I have a bag of crisps?' isn't exactly a come-on."

I fiddle with Drummer's reins until he dances sideways. "I didn't want to scare her off."

Wilkinson laughs. "What kind of school did you go to before you came here? A monastery?"

The burning in my face fries coherent thought. It's only a matter of time before Wilkinson finds out he's not far wrong, that my experience with women is practically nonexistent. But like today, in the pub, when they get giggly and start to flirt, my brain seizes up.

"I think someone's on to us." Herald points down the hill, where a dark figure strides across the playing field in our direction. Ransom, our housemaster.

"Blast!" I say.

"Gentlemen," Ransom says as we pull up around him. "Lost again, I see?"

"Yes, sir," Herald says. "We're sick about missing assembly, sir."

"I can imagine." Ransom turns to me. "Headmaster wants to see you in his office, Varenhoff, after you've put your animal away. As for the rest of you, we can discuss

2

your poor navigational skills in my rooms in fifteen minutes." Ransom turns and heads back to the school.

Wilkinson looks at me. "What you been up to?"

"Don't ask me." I've never been called on the carpet before.

We trail up the hill to the stables. I concentrate on stripping off Drummer's saddle and bridle and rubbing him down until his gray coat is smooth and cool.

"You'd think," Herald calls over the partition, "with the amount of money our parents fork over to send us to this labor camp, they could hire a few stable hands."

"At least we can have our horses with us," I say.

When my father decided the local comprehensive school wasn't doing me much good and the family finances could stretch to boarding school, all I cared about was that Redfield was a school where I could bring Drummer. I've had him since he was a yearling, broke him myself, even though my father said I'd never do it and my mother claimed I gave her her first gray hair in the process. But Drummer and I understood each other from the start, and there was no way I was going to go off to school and leave him behind.

"Oh right, Mary Sunshine," Wilkinson shouts from down the aisle. "And the daily privilege of shoveling out their shit. Or is that what you Rooskies are into?"

I shoot a black look in Wilkinson's direction. "I'm not Russian."

That was another part of the appeal. A distant boarding school meant a fresh start in a place where nobody knew who the Varenhoffs were or cared very much if they did. There's too much history with the villagers back home, and I was never able to make any close friends. At least at Redfield, we're more or less equals.

"C'mon, lads." Herald steps out of his horse's stall and latches the door. "What do you think the head wants with you?" he asks as we cross the stable yard to the school.

"Could be he finally realized he made a mistake letting you in." Wilkinson takes a swing at my head. "This is supposed to be an all-male school, gorgeous."

They fall about laughing, banging on each other's backs as we separate in the back hall. I turn toward the head's office, wondering what's up.

The bus from the railway station dumps me in front of the drive to my house. Apparently, the school forgot to tell my parents what train I was on. Nobody was at the station to meet me.

I stare at a pair of iron gates. For as long as I can remember, those gates have rusted in the weeds behind the derelict gatehouse. Now they're fastened to the stone pillars that flank the drive, and locked.

What's going on and how the heck am I supposed to get in? I heave my carryall over the wall and reach for a handhold. I manage to scramble to the top of the wall and drop into the undergrowth on the other side.

I've still got a half-mile walk to the house, hidden from the road by a dense little wood. I huddle into my jacket. It's cold and a wind has kicked up, swirling dead leaves about my feet and rattling the bare branches over my head.

"Ah, yes, Varenhoff," the head had said when I got to

his office. "Your parents have rung up to say you're wanted at home immediately. Matron is going into town this afternoon, and you can go along with her and take the four o'clock train."

"Is something wrong, sir?" I asked him. I hadn't been home in four months, but I'd just seen both my parents the week before when they'd come up for Founder's Day.

"Well, they didn't say." He shuffled some papers on his desk. "But I'm sure it's nothing serious and you'll be back with us Monday morning."

Nothing serious. It's nearly dark when I make the final turn and see the house lit up like a cathedral. The light streams through the long, many-paned windows and picks out a line of unfamiliar cars parked along the carriage circle.

A party? Not likely. My parents don't throw many because the place is basically a wreck. A National Trust orphan on loan to our family since the forties, it's been gradually falling to bits about us and has eaten most of the family fortune. I climb the front steps and unlock the door.

We don't have the money for the proper staff. But everything in the entrance hall has been polished and cleaned and repaired and now seems like a ghost of itself, a memory of former glory. Except for stacks of cardboard file boxes and various bits of computer under the stair. Something is up. Maybe we're being evicted, which wouldn't be a bad thing. Living here has always felt like living in a fading photograph.

One thing hasn't changed. It's still bloody freezing. The central heat has never worked properly. But there's

5

something else. Though there's no one about, there's a feel of activity. I cross the hall and look into my father's study.

A young man stands by the far wall, studying a huge map of Europe pinned over the paneling. A hundred crazy possibilities come to mind, images of James Bond and American police shows. Maybe I'm seeing things. I blink, but he's still there.

"Who are you?" I stand in the doorway, ready to run if he reaches for his breast pocket. "What are you doing here?"

He turns and his dark eyes narrow for a moment. He's not big or physically powerful-looking. Not much taller or heavier than me. But he looks . . . capable, trained. Maybe it's the military-short brown hair or the clipped mustache or his severe suit. Stiff as a poker, he walks across the room, stops in front of me and makes a half-bow, bending sharply at the waist and snapping his heels together.

"I am Count Stefan deBatz," he says in an accent like Dracula's. A familiar accent. "At your service, Your Royal Highness."

2

"What did you call me?" I laugh a little.

"Your Royal Highness," Count deBatz says. "It is the proper way to address a prince."

"Except I'm not a prince." I shift my weight, wishing he'd look somewhere else. Or blink once in a while. "Maybe you missed it, but our family was chased out of Rovenia when the Soviets took over that little country. That was long before I was born. So don't call me that."

Count deBatz cocks an eyebrow, a sign his facial muscles are functional. "I am quite aware of my country's history, Highness."

We have a little staring contest, but I have to look

away because I'm afraid I'm going to laugh again and it doesn't seem the right time for it.

"Look," I say, "what's going on? How'd you get in here? Where are my parents?"

I look at the strange new maps pinned over the walls, the official-looking papers spread over my father's desk, the blue-and-gold flag that had been in mothballs since Grandfather died, now hung over the mantel, the golden griffin rising over the mountains. It's like an old World War II movie where the Nazis take over someone's house. I half expect to see my parents tied in a heap in the corner, but I'm alone with Dracula.

"Your parents are in London and will return later this evening," Count deBatz says. "You were not expected until tomorrow, Your Royal Highness."

This has to be a joke. But Count deBatz looks fairly grim for someone so young, maybe twenty-six or twenty-seven. The impulse to run was probably a good one.

"Who are you? What are you doing here?" I ask again.

DeBatz pulls himself up—if possible—a little straighter. "I am an emissary from the Rovenian government, part of a delegation sent to invite your father to assume the throne as King Ivor the Fourth of Rovenia."

I do laugh then. This definitely sounds like a bad movie.

"You're joking."

"I don't joke." Big surprise. "The Rovenian parliament passed a resolution to restore the monarchy eleven days ago. The declaration was delivered to your father last week, and his formal acceptance was relayed this morning. He is in London with your mother, filming a speech to be broadcast over Rovenian television tomorrow."

8

He's serious. I grope for a chair and drop into it. If this is true . . . bloody hell . . . It means my life is basically over. I slump forward, my elbows on my knees, my hair covering my face.

"It's not true. I don't believe you."

"You must have known it was a possibility, Highness," deBatz says.

But I never believed it. That was my grandfather's world and my great-grandfather's. Not mine. My great-grandfather was King Idylr II, the last king of Rovenia, who escaped the Soviets and set up a government-in-exile here in England and raised his son—my grandfather—to take up the cause. But when Grandfather died, my father said he wasn't going to waste the rest of his life on a dead dream. I was nine then, so to me it was never any more real than the faded pictures of royal relatives all over my grandmother's desk. All that was in the past. How could it reach out for me now?

"You people fought a bloody revolution to overthrow a Communist government," I say. "Why would you set up a monarchy now?"

"It will be a constitutional monarchy. The king will have no official capacity in running the government."

"But what's the point of that?"

I grew up in England. I've seen what a constitutional monarchy is all about, all show and sham, waving from balconies, living your life in front of crowds of people and on the front pages of tabloid newspapers, surrounded by bodyguards and policemen. I don't want any part of it. I can't believe my father would, either.

"May I sit, Highness?"

9

I shrug. "You don't have to ask my permission."

"Thank you." He sits across from me, his hands flat on the arms of the chair. "Rovenia is a very poor country. There are few natural resources, the coal mines having run out years ago, the timberlands mismanaged. It was the Soviet way, to cripple the infrastructure of annexed nations and make them dependent on their system. And then when the Communists took over after the Soviet breakup, there was so much corruption, things only got worse. Until the workers can be retrained and industries rebuilt, a new source of income is required."

"What does restoring the monarchy have to do with that? Won't it cost money?"

"Rovenia has great natural and historical attractions as well as excellent skiing. It is hoped the restoration will capture international attention, entice tourists to endure the difficult travel, restore a bit of the old-world charm the Communists wiped out."

"Are you serious?" I jump up and deBatz immediately gets to his feet. "All you want is an advertisement for a ski resort!"

"It is more than that." His voice cracks a little. "Under the Soviets, Rovenia did not exist. We were not allowed to identify ourselves as Rovenians. And the Communist regime that took their place bled us further to line their own filthy pockets. We need a reason to rebuild. A monarch would be a focal point, a link to our shared past."

"My father would never buy into that." I pace round the chair.

My father is content managing what's left of the family fortune, going racing and leaving our past where it belongs: in the past. He's not a king.

"Your father understands the challenges and the tremendous possibilities of the situation, Highness."

I turn and grab the back of the chair and lean across it. "Stop calling me that!"

DeBatz doesn't flinch.

"Rovenian protocol dictates how you are to be addressed. In public, I have no choice. In private, you may invite me to address you otherwise."

"My name is Alex."

"Your name is Alexei Nikolas Tibor Ivorovich Varenhoff, so christened in the Rovenian Orthodox Church. Your people know you as Prince Alexei."

"Look, this isn't real. They're not my people. I'm not Rovenian. I was born here."

His eyes sweep over me and a trace of emotion flickers across his features. "You are not English, Highness."

"I'm not Rovenian, either!"

He doesn't know what it's like, to be born and grow up in a place and still feel transplanted. To grow up speaking a language only a handful of people around you know, to celebrate holidays none of your friends have ever heard of.

"The Rovenian parliament refused to grant our family citizenship when Rovenia became independent."

"That was when the Communists were in control. You are a Rovenian and always have been."

"I've never been there. I don't even know what language they speak." He doesn't have to know everything.

"Rovenian," deBatz says. "You will learn it."

"I'm not good at languages." I turn away from him.

"Tvy pa sukin-sen," he nearly whispers.

I turn round before I can stop myself. That's one of the worst things you can call someone in Rovenian. Hearing him use the language that's been like a secret code for our family this way is a slap in the face.

"You learned Rovenian before you learned English," deBatz says. "I can hear it in the cadence of your speech."

"You have no right to talk to me like that!" Even if it was a trick, to get a reaction.

"Now you sound like a prince." His eyebrow rises again. "You might learn to enjoy it."

He's trying to make me angry. I take a breath and let it out slowly.

"Who knows?" I say. "There might be another revolution." I turn toward the door.

DeBatz grabs my arm, white-knuckled, and nearly jerks me off my feet.

"You ignorant little— If you had lived through a revolution, you would not wish for another."

We're so close, I can feel his breath, see a muscle jump in his taut face, his pupils dilating so that his eyes are almost completely black, the brows drawn, making him look more and more like a hawk. His fingers dig into my bicep. I try to twist away.

"Let me go!" I try to sound more commanding than I feel.

The headlights of a car swing past the window. DeBatz's face changes, as though he's been jerked out of a deep and painful memory.

"Forgive me, Highness." He lets go, breathing heavily, two high spots of color in his cheeks. "Perhaps . . . perhaps you would understand my feelings if you knew what restoring the monarchy truly means to our country, what other people have sacrificed for this opportunity."

He waits. I know it's an invitation to ask him questions, but I head for the door, trying not to run. My arm throbs where he clutched it.

"Your Royal Highness, wait."

DeBatz follows me into the hall as my parents arrive with a half dozen people I've never seen before, all laughing and talking. My father, square-jawed and athletic, his head thrown back in laughter, looks as though he could be the king of a ski resort.

When he sees me, his good humor radiates across the hall.

"Alexei!" he booms. "We weren't expecting you home until tomorrow. Has Count deBatz told you the news?"

He's happy. Happier than I've ever seen him. He's *pleased* by all this.

I look up at him.

"Tell me this is all a joke."

3

"Alexei! You're home early!"

My mother comes down the entrance steps, pulling pins out of her bun, her hair spilling over her shoulders in dark waves. If she was in jeans and a sweater, she'd look like Mum. But in a suit and high heels, she looks unfamiliar. Half queen, half Mum.

She puts her arms round me and kisses me in front of everyone. She smells of the cold night and her own particular warmth. I wish I could hold on to her, but not in front of strangers. I step back.

"I'm sorry we weren't here, *dranyin*," she says. "We wanted to be the ones to tell you."

She's breathless, smiling, her gray eyes turning up into crescent moons, her cheeks pink. Everything about her sparkles. She still has a trace of a Danish accent, even though she's lived in England for nearly twenty years. Her father was a minor German prince whose family fled the Nazis and settled in Denmark.

I explain about the headmaster and the early train but leave out climbing the wall.

"It doesn't matter," she says. "You're home now."

"What's going on?" I ask.

Are these my parents? My mum and dad, like all the other mums and dads, coming to school functions, huddled in macs, cheering Drummer and me on at three-day events. Now cheerfully mutating into the king and queen of Rovenia.

My father pulls off his coat and hands it to one of the entourage behind him. "Give us a moment," he says—used to giving orders already—and they fade away. "Let's sit down and talk about this," he says to me.

"Alone?" I look significantly at deBatz.

My father looks from deBatz to me. "Yes, all right. Excuse us, deBatz."

I follow my mother into the study and wait while my father mutters something to deBatz, who mutters back. My father sighs, says "All right, then," and closes the door.

"I gather Count deBatz told you the news." He moves stiffly across the room, as though unsure—no, as though trying himself out, finding out how a king walks. "And you're not exactly thrilled about it."

"Did he also tell you he practically ripped my arm out of the socket?"

"He admits that he lost his temper." My father hitches himself onto the corner of his desk. "And he's deeply sorry."

"He's a raving nutter."

"Emotions are very high right now." My mother curls into an old armchair in front of the desk and tucks her feet under her. "You mustn't hold it against him."

So that's it? Emotions are high and deBatz is sorry?

"I didn't even know why you wanted me to come home," I say. "Then to walk in on all this and be attacked by Count Dracula—"

"I know this is a shock," my father says. "And I'm sorry you found out the way you did. It wasn't how we'd planned it." He glances at my mother.

I look at them, my father crackling with energy; my mother practically purring, curled like a cat in her chair. I've never seen either of them this excited about anything.

"I thought we were done with all this when Grandfather died," I say.

It was all so far away then. It seemed like a game and we just humored him by playing along. Flags and oaths and anthems and stories of a place I used to think he'd made up. When he died, we stopped playing. We still kept Rovenian holidays, went to Easter Mass at the Rovenian church in London, spoke Rovenian round the house, and kept the Varenhoff coat of arms over the fireplace. And until she died three years ago, Grandmother would cook cabbage rolls for New Year's, make us paint and bury eggs on Badenitza Day and fill the house with traditional Rovenian embroidery. But the talk of crowns and thrones was over.

"I know," my father says. "I thought he was kidding himself. When I applied to visit Rovenia after the Soviet breakup and was denied permission, I thought it was definitely history. That's why I didn't push you the way he pushed me, to prepare for something that was never going to happen. Believe me, I was as surprised as you are."

"But why do you have to do it?"

"You know as well as I do that there are no other Varenhoff heirs."

I shake my head. "I mean why can't you say no? You don't have to do it."

"They asked me, Alexei. The restoration was put to a popular vote, and eighty percent of the Rovenian people voted for the return of the monarchy. For the first time since World War Two, they have a real choice, and they chose to have a king. How can I say no to that?"

"It's all about what they want," I say. "They wouldn't let you visit Rovenia, but now they snap their fingers and you're ready to do whatever they say."

"What one person wants isn't always important." My mother uncurls her legs and leans forward, her hands clasped in front of her.

"What if I did say no?" my father asks. "And went on spending my life riding and skiing when I could have assumed this . . . responsibility. This role. I don't like that picture of myself. I don't like what it would say about me."

So this is about his pride? He's got to turn our lives upside down so he can face himself in the mirror?

"Alexei, I didn't jump at the chance to wear a crown. Your mother and I considered very carefully how this

17

would affect you. We know we're asking a lot of you, to give up your life here and take up a role you were never really prepared for. But we will help you to prepare, and we think you can handle it."

"And we would never ask it of you," my mother says, "or put you at risk if we didn't feel we could have a tremendous impact for good."

"What do you mean, at risk?"

They exchange a look.

"Being in a position of high visibility puts us in a certain amount of danger," my father says carefully. "Not every Rovenian wants the monarchy restored."

Right. Like twenty percent of them.

"But all possible safety measures will be taken." My father walks round his desk, too wound up to be still for long. "Security systems, bodyguards, advance preparations whenever we appear anywhere."

"You mean—" My throat goes tight and I can't swallow. "You mean there are people who don't want us there so much that they'd try to kill us? And you still think we should go?"

The past again, reaching out, stories of my great-great-grandfather Tibor blown to smithereens by an assassin's bomb. But that was nearly a hundred years ago.

"I'm saying we've taken every possibility into consideration." He leans across the desk on his broad hands. "The danger is real, I won't lie to you. But we can't let threats keep us away. We're aware of the risk. We'll treat it seriously and take precautions."

I can't believe this. One minute I'm worried about

a detention at school and now I've got to think about someone wanting to kill me? All for what? I blink hard.

"I know it's a lot to take in," my mother says. "But you must trust us and try to understand why we feel we have to do this."

"Why is it wrong to not want to do it?" Because I don't want to. I want to go back to school, be with my mates, go to university, just be like everyone else, not a focal point for a million strangers. Definitely not a target.

"You and your father carry a mythic past in your veins that is important to the people of Rovenia," my mother says. "You are living reminders of what was and what can still be. In a sense, you belong to them."

I've heard this before. My grandfather used to tell me as though it was some wonderful secret, taking me up on the roof of the house to raise his flag. Raising the griffin, he called it.

"Never forget, Alexei," he would tell me, "what this flag means. The griffin has the strength of the lion but also the intelligence of the eagle. He will fight to the death; he will not be taken captive. That is why we went into exile, rather than be taken prisoner. For five hundred years, the Varenhoffs have personified what it means to be Rovenian. That is the treasure you must protect until Rovenia needs it again. You are that griffin and you belong to your people."

That whole idea always gave me the creeps, as though my body isn't entirely mine. Deep down, I've always known it was part of me, but I thought of it as some dead, recessive gene. A little bit of me that had no real impact on who I was. Now it's been brought to life by popular vote. But what if it isn't enough? How strong can that connection be after all these years? How Rovenian am I?

"Try to see it in historical perspective," my father says. "This is enormous."

It is. Enormous, crushing the air from my lungs. I claw at my school tie.

"I know it's overwhelming," my mother says. "But you don't have to grasp it all right now. We won't be leaving for Rovenia until late spring. There are preparations to be made both here and in Rovenia. And the castle is still being updated and restored."

I've been in ancient castles here in England, and they're not exactly the stuff of fairy tales. They're damp and cold and smell when it rains.

But anything could happen in five months. Rovenia could decide to say no again. I can go back to school, where I'm just Alex, and hope for it all to be called off.

My mother squeezes my hand. "Please, Sasha." She hasn't called me that since I was a little boy. "Promise me you'll try."

"Try what?" I stare at her. "I don't know what you want me to do."

"Try to understand the role you are being asked to fill," my father says, "before you set your mind against it."

"Believe that it's a chance to do great good for a country that is struggling to become independent again," my mother says.

I still don't understand how a monarchy could fix that, but I let out my breath. What else can I do?

"All right. I promise."

My father lowers his head so that I can't see his expression. My mother sits back in her chair, smiling.

"Only please don't tell me I've been secretly engaged to some lump of a princess since birth."

4

I wake up the next morning, surprised to find myself in my own bedroom, staring at the familiar pattern of cracks on the ceiling. For a second, I can't remember why I'm here and not at school, why the alarm hasn't gone for me to get up and feed Drummer and clean his stall. Until I remember the fairy godmother in the shape of deBatz, who blew my world apart yesterday.

I sit on the edge of the bed and rub my face. I wonder if I look any different. I don't feel any more royal than I did yesterday morning. Maybe it's a gradual thing. I get up and wash and pull on some old riding clothes. I wish Drummer were here. But my mother won't mind if I ride her horse. I need to get out by myself, do something physical.

I take the back stairs, hoping to avoid meeting anyone, but run smack into my father in the back hall.

"Where are you going?" he asks.

"I was going to take Mum's horse out for a run. Want to come?" It's been a while since we had one of our races through the park.

"I don't think that's a good idea," he says. "In fact, I'd rather you didn't go outside the park or into the village for the time being."

"Why not?"

"We don't want the news getting out just yet."

"I'm not going to tell anyone. I only want to go for a ride."

"Well, there isn't time this morning. We have a lot to do." He puts his arm round my shoulders and steers me down the hall. "There are some people I want you to meet with."

He stops and takes a step back, inspecting me. "Haven't you anything decent to wear? Well, no time to change now. We'll deal with your clothes later. And your hair."

"What's wrong with my hair?" I reach for it, where it curls just short of my shoulders. It's been like this for years and nobody's had to "deal" with it.

But he isn't listening. He's moving on and I trail after him into the sitting room at the back of the house. My mother is there, talking with a woman. Standing by the French windows is deBatz. I stop dead.

"Good morning, *dranyin*." My mother comes and kisses me.

23

"Alexei," my father says in a whole new voice. His king voice. "This is Ellen Ketterman, from the United States. Ms. Ketterman, my son."

The woman steps forward, a blur of sleek blond hair and a trim gray suit. She makes a sort of curtsy and holds out her hand.

"I'm honored to meet Your Royal Highness," she says.

I stare at her outstretched hand, my mouth gaping. What am I meant to do? How are you supposed to react to perfect strangers bowing to you? I feel the sweat break out, thinking of having to face this sort of rubbish every day of my life.

"As you can see, Ms. Ketterman," my father the king says, "Alexei's manners could stand a little brushing up."

Ms. Ketterman pinches her chin and considers me. I look at my father, wondering if he really means it, but can't catch his eye.

"If you'll forgive me, Your Majesty," Ms. Ketterman says in a rapid-fire Yankee accent, "I'd say with looks like this, His Royal Highness doesn't need manners. Most people are willing to forgive an attractive young man almost anything."

My mother squeezes my arm.

"The opposite is also true," my father says. "Many people instinctively mistrust the beautiful."

The beautiful? Does he mean me? He makes it sound like a defect. Why is he suddenly talking about me as though I'm not even here?

"Of course, Your Majesty." Ms. Ketterman nods. "But manners won't change their minds. Others will appreciate His Royal Highness's lack of pretense."

"Well, I suppose it's your job to put a positive spin on things," my father says.

"Her job?" I stare at Ms. Ketterman, who flashes a set of perfect teeth at me.

"Ms. Ketterman is a public relations specialist." My father sits in his leather chair by the fireplace. "She is part of a team that has been hired by the Rovenian government to handle our press and publicity. She will work with you to help prepare you for your public role. She's very qualified as she has a charming daughter your age."

For a moment, Ms. Ketterman's face is blank, as though she hasn't a clue what my father is talking about. Then she shows off her teeth again. "I can't take any credit for Sophy."

"And of course," my father says, "Count deBatz will work with you as well."

The lightning bolts are coming a little too fast for me. I slip my arm out of my mother's and make a wide circle round the cool, qualified Ms. Ketterman to stand in front of my father.

"What do you mean, Count deBatz will work with me?"

"He has accepted a post as your chief equerry," my father says.

"What does that mean?" I glance at the expressionless deBatz.

"He'll be your advisor and counselor. You'll need his help."

Like I need a knife in the ribs. But my father doesn't know this cretin. He didn't see how he treated me yesterday. He can't put me at the mercy of this raving nut.

"Can't you find someone else?" I say in a low voice. "You know what he did yesterday."

My father leans toward me. "Alexei, you're going to have to trust my judgment on this," he says. "There's a lot to do and your mother and I will have our own work. Ms. Ketterman and Count deBatz will help you prepare over the next months."

"But I'll be at Redfield."

He looks at me as though I've just told him I'm leaving for Mars.

"You won't be going back to school."

"But—but you said five months . . ."

"Alexei." My mother crosses the room and stands behind my father's chair. "You'll need that time to get ready."

"But I have to go to school. And Drummer is there."

"I've hired a van to bring Drummer home," my father says.

"But my friends—" I cast about desperately, feeling this, too, slipping away. "And—midterms are coming up."

"For heaven's sake, Alexei!" My father sits up. "I don't care about midterms. Sending you away to school was only temporary until we could work out the restoration details."

"Ivor," my mother says warningly.

I feel as though I've been head-butted. I take a long, shaky breath. That's why they sent me to Redfield. Not because it was better than the local comprehensive, but to get me out of the way while they worked out their plans. And they deliberately chose a school where I could take my horse. They knew I'd come home on weekends if Drummer was here, and they didn't want me to find out what was going on. God!

"How long have you known about this?" I look from my mother to my father.

"Since late summer," my father says.

"Nothing was certain then," my mother says. "That's why we didn't tell you."

"You stuck me away at Redfield and didn't tell me my whole life was going to change!" My hands clutch at nothing. "All that time and you never mentioned it to me, never asked me what I thought until it was too late. I never had a choice, did I? You treated me like a child." I almost stamp my foot. "I'm not a child!"

"Then stop acting like one!" My father smacks the arm of his chair. "Deal with it. Like an adult."

"This has nothing to do with what the Rovenian people want or what anyone else wants except you," I say. "You're as thrilled as Grandfather would have been."

"That isn't true."

"It's only a big ego trip." The words pour out. "Like it was for him. Only you get a real crown and we get bodyguards!"

My father stands up so fast, the chair tips backward and my mother has to step out of the way. His face is barely under control, his skin dark red.

"Apologize now."

But I'm choked with a clot of feelings, all fighting to get out. Why should I apologize when they're the ones who've been keeping secrets from me and making huge, life-altering decisions behind my back?

"Alexei, please." My mother comes to me and puts her hands on my shoulders. "Remember what we talked about yesterday. We did what we thought was best."

But I can't remember. Yesterday is a million years away, another dimension almost. Everything has shifted. Most of all, I can't get used to this stranger my father has become. His altered voice and sudden drive, the new, unfamiliar lines of anger on his face. It's as though he's under a spell and I can't break it.

"Dad?"

"Apologize." His voice is low but charged with an energy I can almost feel, his face still dark red. The room has gone still and quiet. We've never fought like this. I don't know what will happen next.

"May I make a suggestion, sir?" DeBatz's even voice carries across the room. "Why not put His Royal Highness completely in the charge of Ms. Ketterman and myself? At least until we arrive in Rovenia. Give us all an opportunity to become accustomed to these changes."

What a smoothie he is, playing so nice in front of my parents.

My father breathes out, losing some of his color. "Yes, all right," he says, very un-kingly. Then pulls himself up. "I turn Alexei over to you. You have five months to turn him into Prince Charming." He tries to smile at me, but I look away. "You might want to start with a haircut."

"What?" I jerk my head up.

"The hair has got to go, Alexei," he says. "It's far too long."

"No." I brace for another fight. "I'm not cutting my hair."

"Of course not," my father says. "The barber will do that." He's trying to lighten things up, but it's a bit late.

"If I may, Your Majesty," Ms. Ketterman says, "His

28

Royal Highness has fantastic hair. It's a great color, has a good wave to it and really brings out those dark eyes and accents his terrific bone structure. The length presents the sort of young, modern image we're looking for."

Fantastic? Two days ago, my hair was a fact of nature. Now it's part of a modern image, something that could possibly affect an entire country. Something else over which I have no control. Not to mention my bone structure!

There's a moment of silence.

"I don't agree with your taste, but I will trust your judgment," my father says pointedly. "I'll let you get to work." He holds his hand out to my mother. "Minnie?"

That's his pet name for her, from her proper name, Marie Alexandra. A silly name for a queen, but she takes his hand, like a mouse.

"I'll see you at lunch, Alexei," she says. But I can't look at her. I'm too angry with her for letting my father get away with this, for abandoning me.

The door closes behind them and I'm alone with my new watchdogs. DeBatz watches me. If I didn't know better, I'd think he looks sorry for me.

"We'll begin in the morning, Highness," he says.

"Begin what?"

"Lessons. Nine-thirty tomorrow morning, in the library. The rest of today is your own. Make the most of it. After today, we work morning and afternoon. We have a great deal of ground to cover."

29

I **walk straight out** through the neglected garden and down across the lawns to the slope on the far side of the old boxwood maze. I sit and stare at the river snaking along below me, only a few ripples hiding the swift current underneath. Good for drowning. But that's no help. I don't want to be a prince, but I don't want to be dead, either. I want things to be the way they were.

"Blast," I say out loud.

"Is someone out there?" a muffled female voice calls.

I scramble to my feet and look about. The lawns are deserted. I walk to the edge of the maze and look round the corner. No one.

"Who is it?"

"Can you help me get out of here?"

"Where are you?" Someone's playing games with me.

"I'm in the maze." She sounds disgusted. "I can't get out."

I face the wall of overgrown boxwood that stretches over my head two or three feet, and laugh out loud. I can't help it.

"It isn't funny!" She sounds American.

"I know it isn't. I'm sorry. I don't know if I can help you."

When I was six, my grandfather took me into the maze blindfolded and made me find my way out alone. I don't know what he thought I would learn, but I learned I don't like mazes. I'd never gone in again. I'm not about to go in now. Back then, it had been overgrown, tangled with branches that needed pruning. It's probably a jungle now.

"There's a map on the plaque out front," she says. "Go and tell me which way to turn to find the exit!"

"All right." I walk round to the front of the maze, to where the plaque is sunk into a stone-and-cement pedestal, nearly choked in ivy. "Can you hear me?"

"Yes!"

I pull the ivy aside and study the diagram. "Walk forward! And turn right!"

"My right or yours?"

"Oh, sorry! Uh—your left! Turn left!"

"Now what?"

"Keep walking. Take the second left. That's *your* left!"

She rustles through the shrubs. After a bit, she shouts, "There's only one left!"

I look at the map again.

"The other one is almost at the end of the passage you're in. About three feet short of it!"

"Are you sure it's left?"

I look at the maze, trying to see it through the tangles.

"Feel about! It may have grown over."

More rustling. Some shouted curses. A scream of "Ouch!"

"Are you all right?"

"Yes! Now what?"

"Follow the passage! It curves round. Take a left at the top of the circle."

She bursts through the front of the maze, wild-eyed, bits of boxwood sticking out of her light brown hair. There are scratches over her face and hands, and she sits on the ground and examines a tear in the leg of her jeans.

"This is some fun house," she says.

"Interesting way to describe it."

She's American, near my age. Apart from the leaves in her hair, there's nothing remarkable about her. She's rather plump with pale eyes and paler skin. She reaches up and starts to comb boxwood out of her wavy hair with thick fingers. Where on earth did she come from?

"Who are you, anyway?" she asks before I can ask her. Then she claps a hand over her mouth. "Ohmigod! You're the prince, aren't you?"

There's only one answer to that. I nod.

"Rats!" She stands and tries to smooth her tangled hair. "I'm not supposed to say that, am I? I'm supposed to say 'Your Royal Highness' or something. Oh, my mom's going to kill me. We went over this at least a hundred and fifty thousand times."

"Your mother?"

"She's a PR agent. That's public relations. Haven't you met her yet? She said she had a meeting with you this morning. She was really looking forward to it." She stops and stamps her foot a little. "I shouldn't have said that, either. I talk too much."

I try to trace a resemblance between the girl's roundness and Ms. Ketterman's sleek edges.

"You must be Sophy."

"Sophy Campbell." She sticks her hand in front of me, hesitates and draws it back. "Am I supposed to shake your hand or curtsy or what? I forget."

I reach for her hand and shake it; the "how do you do" slips out involuntarily. Her hand is soft and warm.

"What am I supposed to call you? I swear I'll get it right eventually."

"My name is Alex."

She makes a face, squinting at me through one eye. "Really? I thought I had to call you Your Serene Royal Eminent Highness or something."

"God, no. Just call me Alex, please."

Her smooth brows draw together. "I don't think my mom would like it."

"If I give you permission, she can't say anything about it." I wince. "Permission? That was stupid. Sorry."

She smiles at me, a pretty smile, her pink lips spreading back over very nice teeth, her cheeks rounding up like pale apples.

"Can I call you Alex when she's not around?"

She makes it sound like a conspiracy.

"That might be best, as everyone else here seems to think my name's Alexei."

"Isn't it?"

"No."

She considers me for a moment, then says, "Okay, well—Alex, then. Look, I—uh—I've got to go change my pants before lunch. Or is that luncheon?"

She starts to walk toward the house, and I follow her.

"This is some dump you've got here," she says, waving toward the house. "I guess living in a castle won't be much different for you."

"There's one main difference," I say without thinking. "I'll be a prisoner for life."

She stops and looks at me. "What do you mean? You don't want to go?"

"No!"

Sophy frowns. "I thought everybody wanted to be a prince or princess."

"That makes me different, then, doesn't it?"

She looks sideways at me. "Really? I think it would be kind of cool." She says it as though it's nothing.

"What would you know about it?" I snap.

She takes a tiny step away from me. "I don't know. Nothing, I guess."

"Then don't think you can guess how I feel." It's bloody rude, but I can't help it. "You don't know anything about me."

Sophy's cheeks turn pink. "Well, excuse me, Your Royal Eminent Highness. Maybe you don't want to be a prince, but you sure are a royal pain. Guess I'll see you around." She jogs off toward the house.

My face burns. I should call after her and apologize, but she's gone.

The next morning, after a silent breakfast (prepared by the new cook) where my mother desperately tried to draw Dad and me into conversation, I report to the library. I'm surprised to see Sophy at one end of the long walnut table, bent over an open book and a pad of paper. She looks up when I come in, then looks back down at her book. DeBatz stands next to her.

"You are ten minutes late, Highness," he says. "See that you are on time in future. Miss Campbell has already begun her lessons."

"What lessons?"

Sophy reads, her lips moving slightly, idly twisting a strand of hair, ignoring me.

"Miss Campbell has asked to receive instruction in Rovenian history and the Rovenian language several mornings a week."

"Why?"

"To be the better prepared. You might follow her example."

I look at Sophy. "Are you going to Rovenia?"

She gives me a quick, fake smile. "Why yes, Eminent Highness. Though I've heard life in a castle can be pretty dull."

"The correct way to address the prince is 'Your Royal Highness' or 'Highness,'" deBatz tells her.

She turns back to her book and twirls her pencil. "I beg his eminent pardon."

If I didn't believe it was a physical impossibility, I'd think deBatz almost smiles.

"In public, Miss Campbell, please use the correct form." He turns to me coldly. "We will leave Miss Campbell to her work."

I follow him to two stiff chairs on the other side of the room and prepare to sit.

"I am the pope," deBatz says.

I stop, my bottom hovering over the chair seat.

"What?" Has he lost his marbles?

"I am the pope," he repeats. "Do you wait for me to sit down before you can sit?"

"I—I don't know." I straighten up. "Yes?"

"You had better know for sure. Now, let us see how much you know." He doesn't sound hopeful. "In what year was the last of the Mabinov princes overthrown and why?"

The lessons are under way.

6

Nothing I know and nothing I do is right anymore.
In the last three weeks, Ms. Ketterman and deBatz have
driven that home, each in very different ways. Like the day
Ms. Ketterman brought in the ancient little tailor from
London.

"We want to strike just the right note," she said to the
tailor, hanging over him as he crouched between my legs
and fussed over my back, measuring and marking me up
with chalk. "London hip with just a whiff of the halls of
Eton."

I couldn't help doing a double take, accidentally
knocking the chalk from the tailor's hand.

"Your Royal Highness, if you please . . ." He climbed achingly slowly off his stool and retrieved the chalk, muttering to Ms. Ketterman, "You see, when one is not terribly tall, the back is of utmost importance. Every measurement must be exact. I am creating an illusion."

They're all creating an illusion. DeBatz stuffs my head full of boring facts, and Ms. Ketterman tries to create an image. I'm being pieced together out of an assortment of desirable qualities, none of them my own.

I feel cut off from my parents in a way I never have before, even when I was miles away at school. Some days I don't see them at all, and when I do, it's for quick, interrupted meals with people coming in and out and mobile phones ringing. I miss riding with them, going on ski trips, just sitting together in the evening, watching the telly.

But I'm supposed to try, to give this a chance before I make a snap judgment. Which means another morning with deBatz.

In the library, deBatz wipes down a portable chalkboard, his back to the door. Sophy sits at the end of the table, as she did on the first day of lessons, bent over her books. She doesn't look up when I come in.

"If Your Royal Highness will be good enough to be seated, we will begin immediately," deBatz says.

I am good enough and sit and watch deBatz scrawl something in Latin across the board. He pivots on his heel, facing me, and whacks the board with the back of his hand.

"Translate please, Highness."

My Latin isn't all that great, but I say, "To see, to do, to . . . prevail?"

"You don't recognize it?" His eyebrows go up.

It's vaguely familiar. "Should I?"

He points his chalk at the old, battered coat of arms hanging over the fireplace. Like the flag, it shows a griffin rising over a mountain. Under the mountain is a wavy banner with words written on it. The same words on the chalkboard.

"It is your family motto," deBatz says. "Today we will discuss how it illustrates the Rovenian national character."

Damn! I knew that. I think I hear Sophy snort, but she coughs to cover it up.

"Let us begin with Gorba Varenhoff, who chose the motto." DeBatz writes "Gorba" on the chalkboard. "How does his repulsion of the Ottoman Turks from southern Rovenia relate to this motto?"

I stare at him.

"Gorba, Highness." He taps the board.

"I–uh–I'm not sure who that is."

Sophy has another little coughing fit. I want to throw something at her.

DeBatz leans across the table. "Baron Gorba Varenhoff was the father of Arkady, the first Varenhoff king. In 1471, he organized an army of three hundred untrained men and successfully repelled the Ottoman onslaught. Highness, do you know nothing of your family and national history?"

"No, I mean– Yes, I know this stuff, but it's been a while." I concentrate on trying to snap a pencil twined through my fingers. "Ancient Rovenian history doesn't come up much in the British school system."

DeBatz sighs and turns back to the board. "To see, to

do, to prevail." He writes it out in big letters. "The Varenhoffs maintained Rovenia's independence for nearly five hundred years in a region of great turmoil and shifting borders. Topography was on their side, with mountain ranges to the east and southwest. But through battle, treaty or strategic marriage, they prevailed."

He waits for me to respond. Sophy sits up, watching. Heat spreads from my collar over my face.

"So . . . ," I start. "So Gorba basically saw what he needed to do and did it?"

"Basically." DeBatz rubs his forehead. "And he chose this motto and the griffin as a symbol for his family. Do you know what the griffin symbolizes?"

I know this, at least. "It's part lion, part eagle."

"The griffin unites force and industry," deBatz says. "He is brave, independent and fiercely protective of his mountain realm. The Varenhoffs have always seen themselves as guardians of Rovenia. But the griffin is a larger symbol of the determined and independent nature of the Rovenian people. Mountain dwellers—"

There's a knock at the door and a man sticks his head around it.

"Sorry to interrupt, Count deBatz, but there's an urgent phone call for you."

DeBatz sighs again. "Thank you." He picks up a book and hands it to me. "Page seventy-two. The uprising of 1668. Read. I will be back in a moment." He leaves us.

I toss the book onto the table and get up. Sophy scribbles away, ignoring me. We haven't really spoken since that day outside the maze. She's been so prickly, I've been half afraid to apologize.

I stroll down to her end of the table, thinking it would be nice to have someone to talk to. It seems years since I left school, and I miss Herald and even Wilkinson. Do they wonder why I never came back? I haven't been allowed to call or e-mail anyone.

Sophy looks up at me. "Don't you have an uprising to read about, Eminence?"

"I'll read it later." I flop down in an armchair across from her. "I can't believe you're voluntarily listening to this rubbish."

"What else can I do?" she says. "Forced to live in this gorgeous old house with a handsome prince. I might as well make the most of it. Of course, I'd rather be in Pittsburgh with my dad, living in a run-down subdivision and going to a poorly funded high school with asbestos raining on my head."

"Seriously. Shouldn't you be in school?"

"I'm far enough ahead that six months won't matter much. If I decide to stay with my mom, I'll enroll in the English School in Brabinsk this fall. Besides, this is all very educational." She turns an exaggerated wide-eyed look on me. "Why, just think how much I learned about griffins this morning."

"Ha ha. Much good that'll do anyone."

"You never know." She grins and goes back to her studying.

I watch her for a moment. "How's the Rovenian coming?"

"Pretty good." She sits up, holding the book in front of her. "I can say *'Kyahk tyvzha zvoost? Manya zvoost Sophy.'*"

"That's useful. How many Rovenians do you think you'll meet in your life that you'll want to be on a first-name basis with?"

"Besides you?"

"Me?"

"Ye-e-e-s. You are one of the few Rovenians I actually know."

But I have a hard time thinking of myself as a Rovenian.

"And look here." She flips a few pages. "Here's your national anthem. How's it go? 'Follow to the . . . enemy, come . . . answer? Brother?" She stumbles over the words.

"No, no." I laugh at her. "It's 'Come, courageous brothers, the invader to make wet the mountains with his blood.' It loses a little in direct translation."

"Kind of gruesome, isn't it?"

"I always thought it was cool," I say. "And yours is all about bombs and rockets exploding all over the place, isn't it?"

"True," she says. "So how's it go? Can you sing it?"

"I'm not going to sing it!" I say, embarrassed.

"Oh, come on. Please?"

DeBatz's sharp footsteps clap smartly down the hall toward the library. Sophy and I both turn and look guiltily at the door.

"You know," Sophy says, "there's going to be a quiz on that uprising thing."

"Not today." I look around for an escape route. "Do you like to ride?"

Her eyebrows shoot up. "Ride what?"

"Horses, of course."

She makes a face. "Um, well . . ."

"Come on."

I grab her hand and pull her out of her chair, through the French windows and across the terrace toward the stables.

7

"**Alex, I'm not sure** this is such a hot idea."

"It'll be great." I pull on a girth strap. "You've got heels on your shoes."

"Huh?"

"So your feet won't slip through the stirrups," I explain.

"Oh. Well, see, I've never actually been on a horse."

"I promise Sweetbriar's a perfect lady."

Sophy still looks doubtful. "Isn't this your mother's horse?"

"Mmm-hmm." I move on to saddle Drummer, running my hand along his dappled gray neck, the hairs smooth as satin under my hand. He quivers in response.

"I don't think I should be riding the queen's horse," Sophy says.

"She'll be grateful. Sweetbriar's getting soft, standing about."

I hand her a hard hat and lead both horses into the stable yard. It's a mild day, which is good since neither of us has a coat. I hold Sweetbriar by the mounting block.

"Come on," I say to Sophy.

She looks at Sweetbriar, then at me, then back at Sweetbriar. "I don't know . . ."

"We'll take it slowly. I promise."

"The Rovenian character in action," she says.

"What?"

"You. To see, to do, to make people ride horses when they're terrified."

"Just get on the horse," I tell her.

"See? I'll bet that's exactly what old Gorba said to his army."

"I came out here to escape the history lesson." My hand tightens on Sweetbriar's bridle and she tosses her head. Sophy squeals and jumps back. "Oh, come on! It's all right."

"Ooohhh . . . okay. Y'know, all that talk about griffins being determined and independent is just a nice way of saying they're stubborn." She climbs onto the mounting block and lifts a foot to the stirrup.

"Maybe," I say, "but you'd better put your other foot in the stirrup, or you'll end up backward."

"Oops."

"There you go. Now swing your right leg over her back and try not to—"

Sophy drops into the saddle and Sweetbriar dances

sideways, snorting impatiently. Sophy flops forward, trying to hang on to the flat saddle.

"Alex, I don't like this! I probably look really stupid."

"No, it's okay. You look terrific."

"I'll bet. Princes aren't supposed to lie, are they?"

"I wouldn't know." I swing onto Drummer's back, bring him round to Sweetbriar's side and show Sophy how to hold the reins.

"Don't pull. But don't let them slack, either. Keep this much tension." I pull on the reins to show her. "All right?" She nods. "When you want her to go forward, lean forward and squeeze with your calves. You want to try?"

She groans. "Okay, I guess."

"Fantastic! Come on." I urge Drummer forward and Sweetbriar falls into step beside him, probably more out of companionship than anything Sophy's doing. I look at her. "That's good," I lie. "You could try to relax a little. Try to go with her rhythm."

"Are we going somewhere? Anyplace where actual people might see me?"

"No. Only round the park."

"Good."

We ride in silence for a little while. Drummer's impatient, on his toes. He's not used to a decorous pace, expecting one of our wild gallops. Sophy concentrates hard on relaxing, still shifting a little in the saddle with every step.

"So what do you think?" I ask her.

She looks up. "About what? Life in general?"

"No, about riding."

"It's okay. Might be something you have to be—you know—dedicated to."

I consider that, and the horses keep walking. Sophy's all right. It was sort of rotten of me to drag her out of the library and expect her to go along with me.

"I—uh—wanted to tell you I'm sorry," I say, surprising her and myself.

"About what?"

"About what I said when we met. You know, at the maze." I can't remember exactly what I said and hope she doesn't expect me to tell her.

"Oh, that's all right." She rearranges her reins. "I guess everyone thinks nobody knows exactly how they feel. I mean, how could they? But maybe I can understand a little of where you're coming from even if I don't know squat about being a prince."

"Oh? Like how?"

She looks past Sweetbriar's ears. "Well, believe it or not, there are other places I'd rather be." She smiles at me. "No offense."

"Of course." Drummer takes the bridle path along the edge of the park and Sweetbriar follows. "What's your first choice, then?"

"Just a good school, I guess. But I think my mom is hoping I'll be seduced by the glamour of this job. You know. It's the old tug-of-war thing between her and my dad."

"So glamour isn't your thing?"

She laughs out loud and Sweetbriar cocks her ears.

"Oh, come on, Alex." Her smile fades. "I don't know, I feel uncomfortable with all this—" She gestures vaguely with her head, still grasping the reins. "You know, these people, the talk and the pretense."

I look ahead, between Drummer's ears and frown. "It isn't for me, either."

We ride along for a few moments.

"Maybe we were both switched at birth," Sophy says.

DeBatz is waiting in the hall when we come in, his arms across his chest.

"Would you excuse us, Miss Campbell?" he asks.

Sophy wiggles her eyebrows at me.

"I'll see you around." She makes a quick escape. Smart.

DeBatz and I stare at each other.

"Well?" I ask.

"Well what?"

He's too good at this. He seems to know exactly what I'm going to say and always has a ready answer. I can't help being drawn in.

"Go on and tell me how I've wasted the morning and your time."

"That is not what I was going to say, but good points, all the same."

I knew it! He's made me say what he wanted almost as though he's a ventriloquist.

"Then what were you going to say?"

He shrugs and looks at his watch. "Only that you are ten minutes late for our afternoon lesson and that you have missed lunch." He reaches behind him and pushes open the library door. "Shall we begin?"

8

At the end of a two-hour analysis of the Rovenian gross national product, deBatz hands me several sheets of paper, neatly typed, a list of questions, like a test. But the answers are already provided, in essay form.

"What am I supposed to do with this?"

"Read it. Commit the questions and answers to memory."

"What is it?"

"A list of questions you might be asked by the press and the appropriate answers."

I read the first question: "What are Your Royal Highness's goals as prince?" And the answer: "As heir to the throne of Rovenia, it is my duty to serve my people. My primary goal is to find the best way suited to my talents to fulfill that responsibility while preparing for my future role as king."

So they want to provide my thoughts as well as my clothes and my manners.

"This isn't what I would say." I hold the papers out, but deBatz doesn't take them.

"What would you say, then? What are your goals as prince?"

How can I have any princely goals when I don't know anything about being a prince?

DeBatz is watching me. It's like the Gorba disaster all over again, but all I can say is "I—I don't know."

"Precisely why the answers are being provided for you." A corner of his mouth twitches.

"I'm not going to memorize this and pretend it's what I think!"

"Can you come up with anything better?" He leans over my chair, not smiling anymore. "It is my job to make you into the kind of prince Rovenia needs today. I know how to do that. You do not. Everything I try to teach you contributes to that goal. Why not make it easy for both of us, Highness, and do what you are told?"

He straightens and smooths his jacket. "Now take that list to your room or to some other place and study. I have a meeting."

My hand clenches into a fist, wrinkling the smooth pages. I told my mother I would try. If she knew about this, she'd let me out of my promise.

Out in the front hall, I stop a passing woman with a sheaf of papers in her hands.

"Where is my mother?"

"Her Majesty is in a meeting, Your Royal Highness," she says, still on the move. "She won't be free until this evening."

"Iris?" someone calls from the bank of telephones under the stairs. "Relief Aid is on the line!"

"Would you excuse me, Your Royal Highness?" And she bustles away.

I stand there listening to phones ringing and shoes tapping across the floor. This is how it's going to be from now on: strange people running about; having to make an appointment to see my own mother.

I finally find her in the upstairs parlor, surrounded by about a half dozen earnest-looking people, all clutching clipboards or portfolios, a woman talking in a low, fervent voice. The door is open, but I know I should knock.

"Mum."

Everyone round her turns and stares.

"What is it, Alexei?" my mother asks.

"I need to talk to you."

"Can it wait, *dranyin*? I'm in the middle of a meeting."

No, it can't. Can't she see that?

"I really need to talk to you now."

She smiles an apology.

"Do excuse me. I'll be back in a moment."

Everyone stands when she leaves. She propels me into the hall and closes the door behind us.

"Alexei, I want to be available to you whenever I can, but many of the people in that room have traveled long distances and their time is very valuable. They represent large charity foundations that may offer aid to Rovenia." She smiles again. "Now. What was it you wanted to tell me?"

She's being very careful, but I can feel her impatience. I hand her deBatz's questions.

"Have you seen this?"

I watch her bent head with the hair twisted up the way it always is now, her clear eyes flicking back and forth across the pages, my heart thudding, waiting for her to rescue me. She smiles at me.

"But this is wonderful! I knew you would understand what was being asked of you if you tried. It's not so difficult, is it? Stefan must be pleased with your answers."

Can't she tell the difference between deBatz's propaganda and what I might really think? Or doesn't she want to? I take the papers from her.

"These aren't my answers." I turn to walk away.

"What do you mean?" She puts a hand on my arm. "Whose are they?"

"They're Count deBatz's," I say, without turning. "He's telling me what to think, what to tell people I think."

"Oh." She walks round me so that I have to look at her. "Well, can you write your own answers?"

She doesn't get it. I turn my head away.

"The questions are stupid," I say. "I don't have any answers."

She puts her hand on my face and smiles in that way she has, wanting me to smile with her.

"Have you really tried?" she asks. "I know it isn't easy, but think what it means for me. I'm trying too. I don't have the blood ties to Rovenia that you and your father have. I must prove myself in entirely different ways."

I look at her, questions crowding my chest. All the things I should know and feel, that should make me a Rovenian, aren't there. Or if they are, I don't recognize them.

"But I don't feel that tie," I tell her. "What if . . . I'm not Rovenian enough?"

"It's there, Alexei. It will come." She squeezes my arm. "As it will come for me through my love for you and your father. We'll help each other. And Stefan knows what he's doing. Trust him to help you."

DeBatz again. It's pointless. I try to step past her.

"Alexei . . ."

"I'm sorry I interrupted you." My breath comes hard, pumping my chest until I think I'm going to explode there in the hallway.

"I must get back." Her eyes flick over my face. "Please come and talk to me later, after dinner."

She leaves me standing there, my skin on fire. She asked me to try. When I tell her I can't do it, she tells me to trust deBatz. I'm shaking when I push away from the wall and walk off down the hall. I'm on my own. If Gorba Varenhoff could turn back the Ottoman Empire with only three hundred men, I should be able to handle deBatz.

9

I sit facing the coat of arms over the library fireplace. Sophy isn't here, an ominous sign. I rub my arms and stick my hands under my armpits to warm them.

I had breakfast in the kitchen this morning, avoiding my parents. The cook made Belgian waffles for me while she sang along with pop songs on the radio. The kitchen was bright and warm and smelled of bread dough and stewed chicken. Stark contrast to the cold, silent library with the lingering musty smell of the long-gone books.

"Let us see what you have learned." DeBatz strides into the room and dumps some ancient books on a small table in front of me. He picks up a sheet of paper and reads off the first question. "What are Your Royal Highness's goals as prince?"

I stare at the griffin on the coat of arms and say, "Abdication."

DeBatz almost does a double take but catches himself. He moves on to the next question. "How does Your Royal Highness find Rovenia?"

"Turn right at Prague."

"Very amusing, Highness. More amusing still when you are faced by a dozen reporters with microphones and cameras, all recording every word you say." DeBatz lays the paper on the table. "Do you think I make up these things to torment you? I am trying to help you. How you present yourself in public is most important. You must understand that every word you say, every move you make can have far-reaching consequences."

"This is a load of rubbish. It isn't what I think."

"Have you considered the possibility that no one cares what you really think?" He braces his hands on the table. "The media will catch any mistake you make, so you had better prepare. You are not equipped to handle them on your own."

I stare hard at the fireplace. If there was a fire laid, I think I could make it burst into flames.

"Shall we start again?" DeBatz's voice is back to its usual formality. "I believe the question was 'What are Your Royal Highness's goals as prince?'"

He strides to the window and stands, his hands clasped behind his back, waiting. I crumple the pages into a ball and throw them at the coat of arms. It bounces off and drops to the floor. An empty gesture like everything else.

"Pick it up," deBatz says without turning.

"No."

DeBatz comes back across the room, his heels hitting the floor so hard I expect the boards to crack under them. He stands by my chair, breathing audibly through his nose, short bursts of hot air, like a dragon building up steam.

I grasp the arms of my chair and stare up at him, hoping I don't look as worried as I feel. DeBatz is probably master of one of those ancient evil arts he could use to kill you with his fingertips. But he can't kill me. I'm the prince.

"Very well, Highness," deBatz says. "If media relations bore you, we'll move on to the history lessons."

He takes one of the books from the table and thrusts it under my nose.

"Take this. Read it. You will be expected to respond to questions on the first ten chapters by tomorrow morning."

I look at it, about a thousand pages in archaic Rovenian.

"You can't expect me to read all that today! It's too much."

"Forty thousand Rovenians were jailed by the Soviets for possession of books like this, Highness," he says. "Today, roughly twenty-six percent of the Rovenian population couldn't read this book if they wanted to. They are illiterate. Schools are overcrowded and ill equipped. Children don't have shoes, let alone books. So don't tell me how tough you have it."

He pushes the book against my chest. "Take it, Highness. Don't test me further."

What can he do? What can he really do? He can't actually hit me. But if I don't want to sit here all day with him breathing on me, I'll have to take the book. I grab it from him.

"If I ever do become king, my first act will be to have you beheaded."

"Now you begin to see the possibilities," deBatz says, expressionless.

The stables are crumbling, like the house. Inside it's warmer, thick with the smell of hay, dung and horse sweat. I peer down the dim aisle, three long noses poking out of the gloom. At the end of the aisle, Sophy stands with her hand on Sweetbriar's cheek.

"Oh, hello," I say. "Are you waiting for another lesson?"

"Actually, no. I don't think riding is my thing. Sorry."

I shrug. "That's all right." But I'm disappointed.

She reaches out and takes the book from my hand. I'm not even aware that I'm still holding it. "What's this? Are you going to read to the horses?"

"Hardly. I wouldn't torture a helpless animal."

She flips the book over. "Something about Rovenia and history? The Bat has a narrow range of focus, I see. Good luck with it."

"The Bat?" I grin at her. Finally, someone else recognizes his essential creepiness.

She giggles and puts her hand over her mouth. "Oops. I mean Count deBatz, of course."

"He expects me to have it all memorized by tomorrow."

"Maybe he has his reasons." She hands the book back to me and drifts over to Sweetbriar, making a cooing sound.

"Like what?"

She shrugs. "Like it might not be a bad idea to be familiar with the history of the country you're supposed to rule."

"Like it matters what happened a million years ago." I dump the book on the windowsill. "Besides, I already know this stuff."

"Oh yeah, you were really on top of that Gorba story yesterday."

I frown at her, my face tingling. "God, I hate this!" I kick a bale of straw. "I can't believe this is happening."

Sophy scratches Sweetbriar's nose for a minute and sighs. "Alex, I don't want you to think I'm, like, not sympathetic or anything, but you don't have a clue."

"About what?"

"About what a tough life is really like. I don't mean I think I have it any rougher than you do, but I know kids who do."

"You don't know what it's like not to have any say in what happens to you."

"Hello! Alex, what do you think I'm doing here?"

"I'm sorry," I say. "I didn't mean it that way."

"Well, you've got a lot to learn about expressing yourself." She has a way of looking at me—as though she's actually seeing me. I'm not sure that's good.

"So what would you do," she asks, "if you could do anything?"

I stare at her. What *would* I do?

"I mean, really," she says, "if tomorrow, all this just—poof—vanished and you were back to being plain old Alex Varenhoff, what would you do?"

"I don't know." The future had always seemed so wide open before, no rush to decide anything. I walk over to Drummer's stall and he pushes his black velvet muzzle into my hand, looking for a treat. "Something with horses, maybe."

"What, like competitions and stuff?"

"No. I don't like it when it gets all serious, all those keen people barging about."

"You could teach riding."

"Lord no!" I shout, making Drummer toss his head. "That would drive me mad."

Sophy sighs. "What then? Mucking out?"

"Why not?" I shrug.

She laughs. "Oh, Alex, you'd go nuts. I'll tell you what would happen if this all went poof. You'd be like most people. You'd go to college, get a job and muck out stables in your spare time."

I focus on picking bits of straw out of Drummer's mane.

"So what's the diff, if the job is being a prince?" Sophy asks.

"Yeah, but it's not that sort of a job, is it?" I stop picking at Drummer's mane and look at her. "It's not nine to five. It's already taking over everything. I can't go into the village or ride my horse outside the park. And I had to leave school and couldn't tell my friends why. I'm not allowed to contact them. When we get to Rovenia . . . What kind of personal life can you have when you're the bloody prince?"

"Lighten up, Al!" She grins at me. "There are worse things, y'know."

I fold my arms over my chest. She doesn't understand either.

"Some things you just have to learn to live with." She walks over to the next stall and tries to coax a dark bay out of his corner. "What's this one's name?"

"That's Treasure," I say, angry and not wanting to change the subject.

"Your father's?" she asks. I nod. "Y'know, yours ought to be white, for Prince Charming. But gray's all right, I guess, since you're not all that charming."

"Ha ha."

Sophy runs her hands up and down her arms. "It's cold out here. I'm going in." She looks at me. "Are you coming? It's almost lunchtime."

I shrug and fall in beside her, watching the wind tear apart her braid. Impatient, she pushes the wisps of hair behind her ears and sniffles loudly. She frowns a little, her brows drawn together. I wonder if she's really unhappy about being here, and my anger dissolves.

"So," I say, "what do you want to be?"

She stops walking and faces me. "You got me there. I'm not really sure."

"Oh ho!"

She laughs and starts toward the house again.

"I don't suppose you'd believe me if I told you I've always wanted to be a princess?"

10

Between my thighs, I feel the muscles that drive Drummer's legs forward, feel his ribs expand. He moves into his flashy trot, responding to my slightest signal.

"Good boy."

His hooves cut through the dead grass and the smell of earth mixes with the clear air. It's a cracking day for late March. A beautiful day to let him run. I can feel his impatience, his bursting energy. We can almost sense each other's moods. I ought to let him open up, tear across the lawn. . . .

"You are posting on the wrong diagonal," deBatz shouts. "Switch now!"

"I did switch!"

"You did not. Sit through the next stride! *Bozhk maj!* An infant could do better!"

DeBatz has me outside in the bloody cold, training for six different Olympic events at once. He fires tennis balls at me with the deadly accuracy of a sharpshooter and sets a killing pace running the perimeter of the rose garden. I reckon he thinks if he breaks me physically, I'll be willing to sit inside and read his dusty books.

"Again!" he snaps, from the end of a long tether.

I dismount and unhook the longe line from the bridle. It dangles like a fuse from deBatz's fist.

"What are you doing?"

"I know how to ride. I've been riding since I could walk." Even my grandfather thought I was good, and he was a tough teacher.

"You know how to sit on a horse and let the animal carry you about, Highness." DeBatz walks toward me, gathering the wide white tape as he walks. "Whether we can call it riding is yet to be determined. Come, let us try a canter."

I hold Drummer's bridle, his warm breath on my hand, watching deBatz advance.

"Or," he says casually, "we could retire to the library and discuss Rovenia's role in the Prusso-Austrian War of 1866."

I swing up onto Drummer's back.

"Did you hear that?" I turn in the saddle and hear the sound again. *Click-click-click,* followed by a long, soft whirring. "There it is again."

"I heard nothing." DeBatz reaches for Drummer's bridle. "A canter, Highness."

"No, wait a minute."

I gather the reins and kick my horse into a gallop, riding hard for the shrubbery on the edge of the lawn. As we near, the bushes erupt. Three men with heavy black cameras slung round their necks tumble out. They scurry toward the drive like flushed game.

One of them drops to one knee and snaps away as Drummer and I bear down on him. Grinning, he gets up, touches his forehead and shouts, "Much obliged, Your Highness," and disappears into the trees along the drive.

I rein Drummer in so sharply that we skid sideways in the damp grass, sending up ribbons of turf. I turn Drummer and kick him into a gallop back to deBatz. I fling my leg over his back and drop to the ground.

"Those were photographers!" I shout.

"Very observant, Highness." DeBatz reaches for Drummer's bridle.

I feel as though I've been sucker-punched. I push deBatz's hand away and lead Drummer toward the stable.

"We are not through, Highness," deBatz calls.

"Yes we are!" I keep walking. My father has to do something about this. He has to. I cool Drummer out, see him settled and find my father at his desk in the study, surrounded by the usual crowd of strangers.

"You've been told about knocking before entering a room," my father says.

That's as many words as I've had from him in a week.

"Do you know there are photographers hiding in the shrubbery?"

My father turns to the man standing to his left, who leans toward him and murmurs, "*The Daily Standard,* Euro wire service and—er—*Cheers Magazine,* sir."

"Cheers Magazine?" My father cocks an eyebrow.

"A quality publication, sir. They expressed a very keen interest."

"Ah. Good."

"Count deBatz's decision to take advantage of the fine weather and move His Royal Highness's lessons outside has been a stroke of luck." Ms. Ketterman lays several papers on top of the pile. "Prince Alexei has been placed before the public months before we could have hoped. Look, just this week, he's appeared in three national newspapers and several really good photos have been picked up by the European wire."

"That's fine, Ms. Ketterman. Well done, everyone."

Of course he knew. It's part of the whole cruddy plot. Newspapers and magazines litter his desk. Blurry photos of my parents and me shot through car windows. One of my mother buying roses in the village, my father by the dried-up fountain, looking reflective. That one might as well have an alluring slogan, like "Rovenia . . . Experience the Magic" and the phone number of a travel agency underneath.

"I can't believe you let us in for this."

The muscles in his jaw and across his shoulders bunch up for a fight.

"Give us a moment," he says to the people round him.

It's almost impossible to stand silent as they leave. When they're finally gone, I open my mouth, but my father cuts me off.

"Alexei, I don't want to hear it. They only took your picture. It's not as though they pulled your teeth."

"But it was a setup. They were invited."

"Yes, they were invited. They're going to take our pictures in any case. Why not play along, use it to our advantage instead of setting them against us from the start?"

He hands me a newspaper, and I sit down and look at it. The front page shows me playing tennis under the headline "Prince Charming Makes a Smashing Return." Everyone at Redfield is bound to have seen it.

"What a stupid thing to say! It makes me sick."

"I know you don't like it. You don't like anything about this." He pushes back from his desk and stands up. "What do you want me to do? I can't change the fact that people are fascinated by royalty and that the world will be watching us. All I can do is try to make it as easy as possible for you and your mother, whether you believe that or not."

I watch him walk to the sideboard and pour himself a drink. I don't think I know him well enough anymore to know what he'd do.

"I know this is a lot to ask from you, especially at your age." He claps the stopper back onto the decanter. "My God, don't you think I know that? Maybe I was wrong, letting you grow up the way you did. If I'd known this was going to happen, maybe I could have prepared you better."

He takes a long drink. He isn't looking at me and I wonder if he even knows he said that out loud. I almost feel as though I'm eavesdropping, that he's going places I don't want to follow.

"My father and grandfather did what they felt they had to do, living for the monarchy. But I didn't want you to have to grow up the way I did. I saw what it did to my father, trained for a role he'd never fill. I tried to resist it myself." He stares out the window. "It was closer for them. They were born in Rovenia. My grandfather wore the crown. But growing up, I could feel it . . . diminishing. It's different now, being asked back this way."

He laughs a little. "I don't know if your grandfather would have entirely approved, much as he wanted it. He always said that a king must be a father to his people. He wouldn't approve of the children making the decisions."

"He liked to be in charge," I say.

My father laughs out loud and turns from the window. "Yes, but I think even he would appreciate how things have changed and how we have to find new ways of serving our people."

"How?" I ask. "That's what I don't understand."

"Leading by example, for one thing," he says. "Taking the intense spotlight that will be on us and using it to shine a light in forgotten places, making the world notice Rovenia again. And giving our people back their heritage and their pride in our shared history. If we can do that much, I think we can win over those who don't want us there and those who oppose the democratic government. I know you have the courage to do this, Alexei, and the heart."

I wish I was as sure as he is, but it's nice to know he has such faith in me.

"I hope you're right."

He looks at me, very serious. "It won't be easy, and it may be dangerous. We know that. But please believe I wouldn't knowingly put you in harm's way if I didn't think I could protect you or that it was more than worth the risk."

Do I believe him? I don't know. In these familiar surroundings, it's hard to grasp the idea that there are people hundreds of miles away who might want me dead.

"So you see," he says, "we can't let personal considerations like not wanting our pictures taken get in the way."

"Will it always be like this?" It's easier to think about paparazzi than assassins, so I ask, "Photographers hiding in the shrubs in Rovenia, following me about when I go riding?"

His head jerks up and he looks at me as though I've reminded him of something terrible. He looks down at his glass, lifts it and drains it.

"We're not taking the horses to Rovenia." His voice turns sharp. He sets his glass down firmly and looks me square in the face.

"What?"

"We can't take them. I'm sorry."

I laugh a little. "Why not?"

He walks round his desk again and sits down. "It costs too much to transport them and there's no money to repair the stables at the castle."

"We could board them somewhere," I say. "There's got to be a decent stable nearby."

"No. The funds simply aren't available. Believe me, I tried to work it out."

"Couldn't we at least take Drummer? I could pay for it out of my trust fund."

My father closes his eyes, rubs the bridge of his nose. "I found a buyer who will take them off our hands before we leave. It's already settled."

I have to breathe carefully or something will burst. I clench my fingers until they nearly break, hoping to wake up. This can't be happening. Take them off our hands. Drummer? Is he one of those personal considerations Dad was talking about?

"Please. Isn't there some way—"

"Alexei, try to understand—"

"But he's my horse—"

"When our family fled Rovenia in 1945, they left everything behind. They came to this country with nothing. Surely you can give up your horse."

It isn't true that our family came here with nothing. They came with a sizable bank account and a small fortune in jewelry sewn into my great-grandmother's underclothes. But I know better than to remind him of that.

"I could pay for it—"

"No!" He smacks the desk. "How would it look if we arrived in an impoverished country with something as elitist as a pleasure horse in tow?"

How would it look? I push myself out of the chair and stand, shaking.

"So that's what this is all about? It isn't about whether we can afford it. It's about how it would look?"

"Alexei, this is the way it has to be. I'm sorry." My father gets up and paces behind his desk. "I can't deal with this right now. This is all new to me, too, you know. I'm sorry I can't make everything work out the way you want it to, but I've got more important things to think about than your horse, your fights with deBatz and your problems with having your picture in the paper. I mean—look at me!"

He beats on his chest with the flats of both hands. "In less than two months, I've got to go be king of a country

I've never set foot in, and I'm trying to figure out how to do that. So please, could you give me one day where I don't have to think about you?"

We stare at each other. His hands are clenched, his face red, his hair wild over his forehead. He sits again.

"I'm sorry," he says, his voice rough. "This discussion is over. Go, Alexei. Now."

"Dad?" I can still feel Drummer's rhythm, smell him on my hands and clothes.

He puts his hands over his face, his breathing hoarse and shallow. I don't know what to do.

"Dad? Are you all right?"

"Please go."

I turn and run.

11

I collide with deBatz outside the study. My throat is so swollen that I can't talk. I try to get past him, but he grabs my arm.

"What is it?" he asks, staring at me.

"Nothing." I break away, but he follows me into the hall.

"I heard him shout at you. Tell me what happened."

"Why should I?" I can't bring myself to talk about Drummer. So I thrust the newspaper at him. "You knew about those photographers, didn't you?"

He looks at the picture, then at me. "I knew there would be . . . opportunities provided for certain members of the press, yes."

"Why didn't you tell me?"

"Your father asked that you not be told. His Majesty guessed what Your Royal Highness's reaction would be."

"You let me make a fool of myself."

"Nobody let you, Highness," he says evenly. "You didn't have to charge at them the way you did. You handed them a headline on a silver platter today."

Something in my head snaps—I can almost hear it. I lunge at deBatz, swinging, but he blocks my blows with his arms. He stumbles backward but recovers and grabs me before I can hit him again. He spins me round and holds me, struggling, my back pinned against his chest.

"Stop it!" he hisses in my ear. "Stop it! Someone will see you!"

"I don't care!" I twist furiously, but I can't break his hold.

"Come with me."

"No." I thrash about with my legs, try to kick him, but he steps hard on my foot.

"Which one of us can hold out longer, Highness?"

I wriggle, jerking my shoulders, but he's too strong. And then it's gone, whatever drove me. I don't want to fight him anymore. I don't know why I hit him in the first place. I go limp, and he lets me go.

"Come with me," he repeats, smoothing his hair and tugging on his jacket.

"Why?"

"I want to show you something."

Numb, I follow him up the stairs and down the corridor, rubbing my arm where he blocked me. DeBatz opens the door to one of the guest bedrooms and steps aside.

"My room, Highness, if you would so honor me."

It's as shabby as the rest of the house but very neat. Nothing out of place, not a sock on the floor or a wrinkle on the coverlet, no personal effects strewn about. DeBatz crosses the room, pulls a red leather album out of the closet and opens it on the desk by the window.

"If you please, Your Royal Highness." He's excruciatingly polite. "I would like you to look at something."

I reach for the resistance that's kept me going against him, but he's given me nothing to fight. So I stand next to him and stare at a page of photographs. Views of a river, a castle, a bridge, a school grouping. I look at him. What's his point?

DeBatz points to the photo of the bridge. "This is the bridge near Metaslav, crossing the Rivka Arel."

It's a huge bridge high above a river gorge between two mountains. He points to another photo of several dozen boys, ranging in age from ten to sixteen, lined up outside a crumbling schoolhouse, blinking against the sun. I know he has a reason for showing me these pictures. To shame me, probably.

"This is the old state school in Uzyatin. When I was thirteen, my classmates and I were taken from that school to work in the labor crew that built that bridge."

It's impossible to imagine that group of dirty, happy boys working on the vast, dizzying bridge. I try to pick out a young deBatz from the group, but they all look alike.

"I was very angry to leave the school and my education, such as it was, but we had no choice," deBatz goes on in his flat voice. "And I had a secret I could tell no one. I had a deathly fear of heights. Yet each day, I was expected to climb out onto the trusses and weld rivets into that bridge. I knew that when it was finished, there would be another or there would be the coal mines, and I would never go back to school.

"At night, my father taught me from his own memory the lessons his father had taught him, stories of our country and our people that the Soviets and then the Communists had tried to wipe from our hearts. And during the day, high up in the trusses, I would repeat those lessons to myself to keep from thinking how far the drop was, until I knew more than I would ever learn in that school. And I vowed to make use of every moment that I had an actual book in my hands."

He sounds like an old, old man, talking about something that happened fifty years ago, not like someone only ten years older than me. It's hard to remember, sometimes, how young he is. He seems so much older. And in experience, I suppose he is.

"The Hrad deBatz in the Arel Mountains in the north of Rovenia." He motions to a photo of what looks like Dracula's castle. "My family's ancestral home. In ruins, now."

He flips a few more pages and stops, laying his fingers on a photo of a brilliantly smiling young man. It had been torn in half and carefully taped together.

"That is Ulf." He clears his throat as though the name has got stuck. "Prince Ardulf Vrenitzi." He mumbles something else, but I only catch the word *tevrish,* Rovenian for friend. DeBatz once had a friend? He's possibly human? "A cousin of yours, Highness."

I have cousins all over Europe, but I've never heard of this one.

"After the building of the bridge," deBatz goes on, "Ulf was taken into the army. He was sixteen." He lays his hand flat over the photo, covering Ulf's smiling face. "That was the year before the revolt against the Communists began. Ulf tried to run away and join the Rovenian National Army, but he was shot in the back as a deserter. The government did not care that he was a prince."

He's dead? They killed him? I lean forward to look at him more closely, but deBatz turns the page to a photo of himself. Dressed in a tattered, ill-fitting army uniform encrusted with medals, looking very young without the mustache, his left arm in a sling.

"When was that taken?"

DeBatz snaps the album shut, nearly catching my finger. "Just after the revolution." He stares out the window. "You have no idea, Highness, what this is really about. You think it's a farce, but it is far from that. People have died for this."

"For the monarchy?"

He turns and looks at me.

"For the right to choose. For the right to ask you to help them. And you can help them. You can make their sacrifice have meaning they never could have hoped for." His eyes are steady, not hawklike at all. "If you want to."

I have a choice? I try to follow him, but all I can think of is my father's shaking hands and Drummer. . . . This isn't my choice. I look away.

"Don't waste your anger, Highness. Turn it to a better purpose."

How can you waste anger? I want to know why he

showed me the pictures, what he means, but I can't think of the words.

He puts the album back in the closet and turns round.

"In a very short time, we return to Rovenia." The ramrod-stiff deBatz is back. "It is up to you to decide how you go."

He leaves me standing in his room, watching him disappear down the hall. His sharp footsteps fade away.

12

I kick Drummer into a gallop, heading him for a five-bar gate in the park fence. It's a crazy thing to do, but I don't care. I don't care if anyone's taking pictures, either. Drummer sails across the heavy bars and lands hard on the far side, pitching me onto his neck. Scrambling to keep my seat, I let him go, tearing across the open fields, the smell of damp earth sharp in my nose, wishing we could go on this way forever.

At this moment, I'm free. I could disappear. They'd look for me, but I know places where I can hide. I haven't any money, but I'd manage. Maybe Herald would help me. I could go someplace where I could get lost and be Alex again. To the West Country. Or even as far as Ireland. Get a job mucking out.

I throw back my head and shout wordlessly, but the sound is torn away by the wind. Drummer slows to a trot, and we ride along the edge of the village. On the church common, two of my old mates from the local school lounge across motorbikes. I lift my hand, but they only stare at me. Then one of them flips me the finger.

I turn Drummer sharply away from the village and follow the river to the co-op fields, where I let him gallop again. I hunch on his shoulders, out of the wind, his mane whipping across my face, not caring where we're going, only wanting to run and not think about anything anymore. But Drummer stumbles, regains his footing and stumbles again. I sit up and rein him in, looking round to see where we are.

We've come full circle and are on the hill overlooking the house. I slip off Drummer's back and sit in the grass, my elbows braced against my knees and my face in my hands. It's cold and windy, but I hardly feel it. The sense of loss and confusion so great, so heavy, I expect it to push me into the earth. There's no escape. Not even temporarily. I should have known.

I get up and lead Drummer down the hill and across the park. At the back garden, we run into Sophy.

"Hi!" she says. "I'm going into the village for a soda. Nobody here seems to believe in Coke." She rubs her mittened hands together. "Want to come?"

I shake my head and fiddle with Drummer's reins.

"What's wrong, Alex?" Sophy asks, her mittens pressed together.

"Nothing." I curl my hand round Drummer's warm, velvety nose.

"Come on. I know it's not nothing. Or is it more of the same thing?"

"Oh right, that." I reach for Drummer's bridle, to lead him past her.

"I'm sorry." She puts a hand on my arm. "I didn't mean that the way it sounded."

"It's all right." I start forward again and stop. I have to talk to someone. "Remember you said being a prince was something I'd have to find a way to live with?"

Sophy nods.

"Well, it's more than that." I look down at the reins twined through my fingers. "It's as though this prince I'm supposed to be—" I take a breath, shift my feet. "He's like someone I don't know that I'm supposed to let take over. Where does that leave me?"

"You're still there," she says. "This prince guy isn't taking over. He—he's just a mask you have to put on."

"I don't think it's that easy. It's affecting everything." I lay my hand on Drummer's cheek. "Did you know I can't take Drummer to Rovenia?"

Sophy's mouth forms a little *o*. "I didn't know. Why can't you take him?"

"Officially, it's too expensive," I say. "But the real reason is that it wouldn't look good. My dad called him an elitist symbol." I laugh to cover my breaking voice.

"Oh, Alex, I'm sorry." Sophy's eyebrows pucker with worry. "Oh. Here."

She puts her arms round me and squeezes. Her down jacket is thick and soft; it's like being hugged by a warm pillow. I let myself sink into it. She lets go and steps back, her cheeks pink.

"I know that doesn't help," she says, "but I didn't know what else to do."

"It's not the worst thing that happened today," I say, heat spreading over my own face.

"Well, that's reassuring." We both look at our shoes for a moment. "Are you sure you don't want to come into town with me?"

I shake my head. "Thanks."

"Want me to bring you back a Coke?" She smiles. "The caffeine might help."

I almost laugh. "No thanks. It's bad for your teeth."

"Right. I guess you have to think about that. I mean, at least you can have the teeth of a prince."

I do laugh, a little. "Thanks, Sophy."

"Don't thank me. Thank your dentist."

"No, I mean it."

She shrugs. "No problem. Whenever you need trivial banter, I'm your girl." She stands smiling at me for a moment and then heads toward the village.

I gather Drummer's reins and lead him to the stable. I'd like to believe Sophy's right, that the prince thing is a mask I can put on and take off. But plain old Alex doesn't exist anymore. I'm Prince Alexei Varenhoff, inextricably connected to those boys who built those bridges, that unknown cousin shot in the back. And to the country they fought and died for.

DeBatz asked me to help them. But he's really asking me to give myself to them. Not the way my father thinks, with a sacrifice here and there. It's deeper than that. I can feel it, reaching inside me, the long fingers spreading out to every nerve, the gene switched on. I don't know what will be left of me—of who I thought I was.

13

When I was little and the stories were only stories, I used to imagine what Rovenia was like. The craggy mountains with their snowy peaks and black pines, the lowlands with velvet hillsides and deep forests full of bears and stags and wild boars. I pictured the towns and villages and cottages. Now it rolls out beneath our small private plane, so much like the stories but all mixed up in the reality of why we're here.

"Brabinsk, the capital, is over those mountains." De-Batz leans past me and points through the window. "There is no skiing in these western slopes." He's talking a mile a minute. "A survey is under way to determine the cost-effectiveness of reopening the coal mines. We are also looking at means to open new industry. Here in the plains, the old agricultural practices are being reintroduced, vineyards and crops of roses for attar of roses, once a major export to the perfume market."

DeBatz excited is a scary thing. It never occurred to me that he might have been homesick those months in England.

"That sounds promising." I sit back, away from the window and deBatz's arm, hoping we land soon. Since he showed me those pictures, we've had an uneasy truce.

Sophy, seated next to her mother in front of me, turns and makes a face at me over her shoulder.

The plane banks sharply, approaching the airport. We land with a bump and taxi to a stop behind a plane carrying my parents and their retinue. My father and I are not allowed to travel on the same airplane in case one of us goes down in flames.

Sophy and everyone else has to stay on the plane. I turn back to look at her, but deBatz herds me down the steps and across the tarmac to wait by the other plane for my parents. I crane my neck to look about, but there isn't much to see. We're on a vast open field, with only the runways and the ugly, utilitarian terminal in view and one road stretching to the east and west. Nothing like the complex motorways round the airport in England.

In the distance, the foothills rise with the gray ghosts of the Arel Mountains hovering above them. It's so different . . . not just the mountains . . . I sniff the air, but all I smell is jet fuel. And overhead is the same blue sky.

DeBatz stops before a line of hulking men in identical dark suits.

"Bodyguards," he supplies. "From an elite squad in the Rovenian army."

Two of them step forward and salute smartly. They both tower over me and probably outweigh me by ten stone each, all of it muscle. I suddenly feel as though my body needs guarding. But it's best not to think about why they're really here.

"Your Royal Highness," deBatz says, back to his formal voice. "May I present your personal detail, Sergeant Major Malek Stepanij and Corporal Jiri Chlebak."

In turn, they shake my hand and mutter "Your Royal Highness."

I have to tilt my head back to look in their eyes, facing a quantity of square jaw and broad neck. The sergeant major is slightly older, darker. But the sandy-haired corporal is bigger. He also hasn't learned how to regulate his grip. I try not to wince.

"How do you do?" I say, sensing deBatz's relief that I remembered how to respond. I wish the men had name tags. I already can't remember which is which. They take up places a few steps behind me. Body guarded.

Across from us stands a group of men and women, their attention fixed on the door of the first plane. Beyond them is a knot of photographers and reporters and television cameras. Two Rovenian soldiers step forward and unroll a narrow red carpet from the base of the airplane stairs.

My parents appear at the top of the steps. My father looks more like a film star than a king, but my mother is beautiful in a neat, plain dress, holding on to a little hat with one hand and my father with the other. My father waves, and the little group applauds, the sound clattering across the airfield like a flock of birds taking off. My parents descend together and stop next to me.

My mother kisses me and stops, her hand on my cheek. "All will be well."

"Alexei," my father says out of the side of his mouth, "try not to look as though you're headed for the guillotine." He takes my mother's hand. "My dear, we're home."

"Ivor." She smiles her dazzling smile. Someone dumps an armload of flowers on her. Camera shutters open and close furiously. My father leads her down the carpet.

"Go," deBatz mutters.

I follow my parents along the carpet to where the honor guard waits, bearing the Rovenian flag. It's larger and newer than Grandfather's, glowing in the sunlight, the golden griffin undulating in the breeze. What would Grandfather think, to see it flying over Rovenia again? A young soldier—not much older than me—holds the flag, stiff in his ill-made uniform, staring straight ahead. I wonder what it symbolizes to him.

My father stands at attention and salutes smartly.

"Now you," deBatz whispers.

I raise my hand to my forehead, self-conscious. Not because of all the people staring at me but because of the young soldier holding the flag and Malek and Jiri behind me and dead cousins and little boys and bridges and a blue-and-gold flag snapping in the breeze. So much seems to be riding on that griffin.

Across the field, three ancient black Bentleys with

miniature flags on their hoods are lined up in a motorcade of policemen on motorcycles and an army truck full of sharpshooters. I climb into the first car with my parents, finally free of deBatz. I turn to the window as the car starts with a quiet rumble, pulls away from the airfield and up a curving road into the mountains.

The road is narrow and full of potholes, no guardrails on the steep overhangs. But the driver doesn't seem to mind. The car swoops along through a forest of tall, slim trees. The sunlight shines through pale green leaves, glows against satiny white bark and falls on a vast carpet of blue flowers and moss underfoot. I almost have to physically take hold of myself.

"I never imagined it would be this beautiful," my father says.

My mother reaches over and takes his hand. He turns to her and they stare at each other. I feel as though I shouldn't be here, shouldn't be looking at them. I face my window, slipping down in the seat as miles and miles of splendor sweep by.

14

The motorcade pulls into Arkady Square in Brabinsk at noon, the ancient bells of the basilica pealing over the city. What I've seen of Brabinsk from the car isn't what I expected. It isn't one of those cramped and crumbling medieval towns. And it isn't one of those industrial cities with horrible blocks of cheap apartments, like giant filing cabinets for people. It looks . . . well used and carefully kept.

I know—because deBatz pounded it into me—that the square is celebrated throughout Europe for its design. On one side, the Cathedral of St. Florian faces the parliament building, flanked by the Winter Palace and a modern hotel built on the foundation of a much older building. The main streets of Brabinsk radiate from the square like the spokes of a wheel. In the center, a battered equestrian statue of King Arkady (hidden from the Soviets at the bottom of Lake Pozni) rises out of the crowd of Rovenians that covers every other inch of space. Only the street that passes in front of the parliament is clear to let us through. The three big cars pull up to the steps and stop.

The cheers of the crowd beat against the car. Arms reach toward us, hands clutching little blue-and-gold flags, reaching, grasping across the crush barriers. Even held at a distance, the crowd seems to press in on us. I can't breathe. It's as though no air can get through that mass of people.

The crowd goes quiet and someone opens the door of the car. Under the pealing of the bells, a strange silence hangs over the square, a collective holding of breath. My father turns to my mother.

"Are you ready, Minnie?"

"Yes, *dranyin maj*," she whispers.

But they sit, staring at each other, hands clasped as though they're about to jump off a cliff. My father looks about to faint. Maybe he's reconsidering. Finally, he steps out of the car. As soon as his dark head clears the roof, the crowd erupts into cries of "Ivor! Ivor!" He turns toward the square and does something that I can't see. The crowd cheers again, chanting *"Kavrol! Kavralyva!"* King and queen. He holds his hand for my mother, and with a quick squeeze of my hand, she emerges to more cheers.

The thought of being pounded by the noise of the crowd keeps me in my seat. There has to be some trick to block it out, but I haven't got a clue. Of all the trivial things deBatz and Ms. Ketterman taught me, they never taught me how to deal with this.

And then the door on my side of the car opens.

"Don't be afraid."

I whirl round, coming almost nose to nose with deBatz.

"I'm not!"

I look out at the lines of policemen facing the crowd, alert for anything suspicious. Army snipers stand on the roof of the hotel and the Winter Palace.

"You will be fine. Go!" DeBatz pushes me toward the other door.

Furious, I stumble out after my parents. I straighten and the tone of the crowd goes up several octaves until it's more of a scream than a cheer. Girls. Early on, I thought this might be the one perk of the job. But the desperate shrieking crashes over me and over the flimsy metal barricades and handful of police officers.

"Come, Alexei," my father calls, and I practically run up the steps to cower behind him and my mother, standing on a broad portico in front of the huge double doors. The prime minister and a throng of severe-looking people step forward.

The prime minister, a short, thin man with bulging eyes and thick lips, stands next to my father, the sun glinting off his bald head and dozens of ribbons and medals glittering on his chest.

"*Luzhta, kavrol maj!* Welcome!" He bows before my father.

My father kneels, bends prostrate and kisses the stone

beneath us. The noise from the crowd swells to a roar, ricocheting across the square, from building to building, deafening. I watch him, stunned. Had he practiced this back in England? I hope he sucks up a bug. From behind and below us, camera shutters click like invading insects.

My mother comes forward and my father rises, kisses her hand and holds it high in the air. The crowd roars again, dizzying. I wish I'd eaten on the plane. I can't pass out here on the steps. I take deep breaths.

The prime minister speaks and presents my father with some order of something or other. The crowd cheers. The Rovenian army stomps by. The crowd cheers. An honor guard presents the Rovenian colors. The crowd cheers.

The Rovenian army band plays the national anthem. The crowd joins in, thousands of people singing about defending their homeland with their last breath. I've never heard it like this, sung by so many people. Even though the words are about something that happened hundreds of years ago, they make it sound as though it only happened a few years ago, to them. And in a way, it did.

My father steps up to a battery of microphones that covers half of his face and strains to see over them. He seems—I don't know—fragile.

"My deepest gratitude for your welcome." His amplified voice booms across the square, strong and resonant. "I have come to reclaim nothing, no throne, no title. I come to offer myself to you, the people of Rovenia. I accept with great solemnity of purpose the honor of serving you to the best of my ability. Though my foot has never before touched this land, my heart has ever been with you, my people."

The Rovenians go crazy. *"Dlinjiv zhyd Kavrol!* Long live the king!"

Lots of them are crying. A television camera sweeps the crowd, the reaching hands, clutching handkerchiefs and flags, the tear-streaked faces. Thousands and thousands of people, crammed together in the square, all yearning toward one man. I follow their eyes and hands to my father, standing so calmly against this wave of devotion. If he's nervous or frightened, if he has any doubts about himself, you can't tell. There's a strange fullness in my chest, and when I try to swallow, it fills my throat.

And then he raises his arms over his head and waves, not a reserved royal tilt of the hand. He waves his whole arms, his whole body. And the Rovenians wave back, still roaring with joy. He knows exactly what to do. He *is* a king.

It's past midnight when the Bentley finally tools up the mountain to Hrad duv Varenjov. Lit inside and out, the castle looms over the city like a golden vulture on the side of the mountain. The night and the strange angle of the lights make it more fantastic and unreal than it is. All that's missing is the howling of wolves and a good thunderstorm.

Inside the walls, I stumble out of the car. We had dinner at a formal banquet hosted by the prime minister. The stewards were generous with the wine, which is probably not a good thing when you haven't eaten much all day. The wine was disgusting at first but more appealing with every glass, spreading a warm looseness through my body and making everything seem very amusing. Particularly the fact that deBatz was seated at the far end on the opposite side of the table and could only glare at me.

Now I'm struggling to keep my feet under me, and it's not amusing at all. I want to lie down somewhere cool, preferably someplace that isn't spinning. But the castle steps look like the Matterhorn. I'll have to crawl on all fours.

"For God's sake," someone—I think it's my father—says. "Help him up the stairs, Malek."

Hands under my arms, hauling me up and into the great hall. A dizzying impression of soaring space and large stone pillars. Far, far away, my parents shake hands with some faceless people. No one pushes me or prods me, so I stay where I am, wavering slightly, catching wisps of conversation.

"Very best wishes . . ."

"A pleasure, indeed."

"Twenty-five years? How marvelous."

"The restorations are nearly complete."

"Many treasures have been restored. And of course, the famous catacombs have never been touched. Every Varenhoff from Gorba in 1474 to Tibor the Third is buried there."

Tibor, my great-great grandfather . . . blown up by anarchists. . . . Wonder if they buried all the bits. . . .

"Have someone show His Royal Highness to his rooms."

A not-unpleasant feeling of being dragged up even more stairs and down a long corridor with walls that seem to move. No, not moving. Hung with tapestries that waver as we pass. A large room and a monstrosity of a bed on a raised platform. More hands stripping off my clothes and helping me slip between stiff, cold sheets. Lights go out, and I'm left in quiet and darkness.

Still spinning, I lie flat on my back. The bed is so high, rolling out of it could cause major injuries. The heavy drapes suffocate, holding in the same musty odor that permeates the whole castle, the smell of five hundred years of Varenhoffs rotting away below me.

Ugh! I pull a pillow over my face, but that smells, too. I'm too tired to think anymore. I roll over and close my eyes, feeling a swell and pitch, as though I'm on a boat. Somewhere, a door slams shut, the latch falling into place with a heavy click.

15

"Highness?"

Someone must have glued my eyes shut. I struggle to open them.

"It is nearly eight-fifteen. Their Majesties are waiting for you in the dining hall."

I squint against the sunlight that pours through leaded gothic windows, throwing a pattern of blue and white diamonds across the floor and bed.

Where the hell am I? I close my eyes, but the light pierces through my eyelids until something looms up to block it. Opening my eyes cautiously, I look into a round face, the small features puckered into worry.

"Who are you?" My voice comes out in a croak.

"Basric, Highness. Your valet."

I groan and roll away from the light and Basric. "Go away," I mumble into the smelly pillowcase.

"But Your Royal Highness's bath has been drawn. It will become tepid if you do not get up at once."

My bath will become tepid? I must still be dreaming. Or drunk.

I burrow deeper into the coverlet.

There's a heavy creaking and the bang of a massive door against a stone wall.

"Is there some difficulty, Basric?"

DeBatz.

"His Royal Highness does not wish to take his bath."

"His Royal Highness knows by now that his wishes do not concern us."

I feel deBatz coming closer, sending out menacing vibrations.

"*Padmitsa, Vreshyniz.*"

"No."

"Get up!" With one yank, deBatz strips the coverlet and sheet from the bed.

I sit up and my brain rolls over with a clanking thud. I brace my hands against the mattress to keep from falling over.

"Get out!" I say when my vision has finally cleared. "I don't want you here!"

DeBatz carelessly rolls the bedclothes into a ball in his arms.

"With all due respect, Highness." He puts a heavy emphasis on the word *due*. "Until your father informs me otherwise, this is my job. Now get up and get in the bath before I pick you up and throw you in myself."

He tosses the bedclothes onto the floor and stands with his hands on his hips.

"I'm going." And when I'm done, I'll have a little talk with my father about deBatz and his so-called job.

I stand unsteadily next to the bed. Even in June, the stones are cool under my feet. I follow Basric to the bathroom adjoining the bedroom.

"Where's the shower?"

"Excuse me, Highness?"

"The shower," I repeat. "Where is the shower?"

Basric points at the long, uncurtained tub. "There is the bath, Highness."

"How am I supposed to wash my hair?"

"That is why I am here, Highness. To assist you."

"I don't think so." I stare at Basric across the bathroom and he stares back, not getting the hint. "Do you want something?"

His mouth opens and closes. "I—I—" He pulls himself up, smoothing the thick white towel over his arm. "My job is to assist Your Royal Highness in your daily functions."

"My what?"

Basric stares past me. "Bathing, dressing, undressing, changing, packing, the care of your clothes and habiliments, care of your person, and miscellaneous duties as needed. Would Your Royal Highness like me to list them all?"

I frown at him. So I've got a new sparring partner.

"Look, I'm sorry, but I don't need your help. Do you mind?" I wave at the door.

"The pajamas first, Highness." Basric steps forward, reaching for my pajamas.

I look at my unfamiliar shirt and clutch a handful of blue silk. No way is this strange little man going to take off my pajamas.

"Go, please."

"As you wish, Highness," he says in a tight little voice. He thrusts the towel at me and leaves the room.

I pull off the pajamas, the silk strange against my skin, and leave them in a blue pool on the floor. I step into the tub and recoil. The water isn't tepid. It's cold. I try the hot-water tap, but only a thin stream of lukewarm water comes out. So much for a fairy-tale existence.

After I finish, I step out of the tub and rub hard with the towel, trying to warm myself. I don't realize until I've dried everything but my hair that I don't have any clothes to put on and that I'm standing on the expensive pajamas, now a sodden, wrinkled mass under my feet. I smother a twinge of guilt about the pajamas, wrap the towel tightly round my waist and open the door a crack.

"Where are my clothes?" I call through the crack.

A stripe of Basric's face appears at the door and I feel his hand on the knob. When he pushes, I push back. The door wobbles but stays between us.

"Open the door, please, Highness."

"Just hand me my clothes."

"I must help you dress." Basric sounds near to tears. "Understand, Highness, it is my job. How you are turned out reflects directly upon me."

My hair trickles cold little streams of water over my shoulders and down my back. I am not going to be dressed and bathed as though I'm a doll. But I'm stranded in the bathroom, wrapped in a towel. My clothes are on the other side of the only door. Basric can't knock down the door. Stalemate.

"Dhvu," a voice spits in disgust.

Blast. I forgot about deBatz.

"The game is over, Highness," deBatz says. "You can't stay in there all day."

"Both of you leave; then I'll come out."

Basric makes a squeaking noise.

"This behavior gains you nothing," deBatz says. "You only waste time and energy, ours as well as yours."

I turn and lean against the door, feeling it close and catch. I'm not trying to gain anything. I only want to dress myself. Is that so much to ask?

"If you are not out in ten seconds," deBatz says, his voice muffled by the door, "I will have Malek and Jiri break down the door and hold you while Basric dresses you." A pause. "The choice is yours, Highness."

That last shot is too much, to suggest I have any choice at all. The bastard. He's got to go. My father has to listen to me. But if I want to talk to him, I have to get dressed. I fling open the door and glare at Basric and deBatz.

It's hard to look threatening in a damp towel.

"For God's sake, let's get this over with."

16

I had no idea putting on clothes could involve so much pulling and tugging and smoothing. By the time I finally make it to the dining hall, I feel as though I've been upholstered rather than dressed.

"Good morning, *dranyin*," my mother says from the end of a long banquet table. "How did you sleep?" As though it's any other morning, not the morning after the world turned upside down.

"Morning, Mum, Dad."

"Good morning, Alexei." My father frowns at me over his coffee.

I make my way round the table, past two liveried

footmen at either end of a sideboard covered with silver dishes, wondering how best to work up to the Fire DeBatz campaign. My stomach rolls at the smell of food, but whether it's hunger or nausea, I can't be sure. I reach for a heavy, carved chair, but one of the footmen is right behind me and pulls it out. I sit awkwardly, the chair bumping into the backs of my legs, and the footman backs silently away. There are odd little royal surprises like this at every turn.

All the furniture is massive, carved within an inch of its life. The furniture of a country with lots of big trees and people with centuries of carving skill. The table is something else, an enormous, gleaming slab, the legs carved in the shape of the familiar griffin. I run my hand along the row of oak leaves carved on the edge of the tabletop and wonder if the person who carved it knew he was carving it for kings, wonder how it survived this long.

My father makes a motion with his hand, like a king in a play, and one of the footmen steps forward, like a footman in a play.

"Ask the chef to prepare a fresh meal for His Royal Highness."

The footman bows and backs out of the room. I watch him go, thinking he'll bump into something. But he makes it to a door hidden in the dark paneling and disappears through it unscathed. How many little doors like that are hidden in this place? Or secret passages. That might be useful information.

"When we settle into our routine," my father says, "breakfast will be at seven o'clock. If you are late, you don't eat. The kitchen feeds more than two hundred people at every meal. You can't expect them to prepare a hot breakfast for you at your whim."

"It wasn't my fault," I say. "It was bloody hard washing my hair in the bathtub."

"That's what you have a valet for," my father says.

"I don't want a valet. I can dress myself. And if I had a shower stall, I could wash my hair by myself."

"You're not getting a shower stall," my father says. "It's too expensive to do any more plumbing in the castle right now."

"Once you begin making public appearances, you will need a valet," my mother says. "Your schedule will be tight on those days. He'll know what you need to wear and how to wear it."

I stare at the dark, shiny surface of the table.

"Alexei," my father says. "Every detail of this business has been carefully considered. If you have a valet, it's because you need one. The subject is closed."

The hidden door in the paneling opens and the footman backs through carrying a covered platter. We stop talking as though the other footman hasn't been standing by the wall the whole time, hearing everything we've said. The first footman places a steaming plate of funny-looking eggs, thin little toast triangles and some sort of shriveled sausages in front of me. He turns to the sideboard and returns with silverware, a cup of coffee, a small bowl of strawberries and a minute glass of orange juice.

The food smells better than it looks. I take a bite of eggs and gag on the unexpected taste of clove. I wash them down with the bitter coffee.

"It's a local specialty," my mother says.

I decide to concentrate on the toast and strawberries.

"What do you think of the castle?" my mother asks. "It will take a bit of getting used to."

A bit. Normal people don't live over the decaying bodies of their ancestors. It ought properly to be made into a tourist attraction, open to visitors on weekends for four *dashkas*. But I catch my father watching me, waiting to hear what I think.

"I haven't really seen much of it."

"We'll arrange a tour," my father says.

I wonder what Sophy thinks about it, the stone floors, the poor plumbing, the smell, the footmen like living statues along the walls. I wonder if she thinks about her own home at all, if she misses it. I think of my mates at school and Drummer. . . .

My father looks at his watch. "Minnie, we ought to be going." He stands.

"Wait!" I haven't had a chance to work round to the deBatz problem.

They both stare at me.

"What is it, Alexei?" my father asks. "We have a meeting at nine o'clock."

"There are things I need to talk to you about."

He sighs. "No shower stall and you will let the valet dress you. At least for public appearances."

"It's not that." Basric is nothing compared to the real problem. "It's deBatz. Can't you please find someone else to do his job? I mean, do I really even need him anymore?"

"Of course you need him," my mother says.

"It's a demanding job," my father says. "You know that

deBatz will be taking on your schooling as well as handling traditional equerry duties. It would be difficult to find someone else who could do both."

"So find me a regular equerry and let me go to regular school."

"A traditional school simply won't fit in with your appearance schedule." My mother reaches toward me across the table. "You know we'd rather you didn't have to make public appearances until you're older, but we don't have that luxury. We all have to take an active role to make this work."

I knew that. Of course. We'd talked about it. I would be tutored around my appearance schedule until I was eighteen. Then I would go to university. Eighteen! More than a year of deBatz.

"There has to be someone else," I plead. "Can't you try?"

My father checks his watch, sighs. "We're very lucky he agreed to take the post at all. I'd appreciate it if you didn't do anything to antagonize him and make him resign."

"But he hates me!"

"Alexei, he doesn't hate you," my mother says.

"You don't see it." I lean forward, my hands gripping the edge of the table. "He's very careful in front of you, but you don't see how he treats me when we're alone. Upstairs just now, he threatened to throw me into the bathtub."

My mother smothers a laugh.

"It isn't funny!"

"I'm sorry, dearest."

"Don't shout at your mother!" My father shakes a finger at me.

My mother puts a hand on his arm. "Ivor, don't. Alexei is upset."

"I don't care," he says. "I don't care if deBatz threatened to throw him out the window. He probably had his reasons." He looks at me. "If you do anything to screw this up, I'll throw you out the window myself. DeBatz stays. No more complaints." He checks his watch again. "Now we're late." He holds his hand to my mother. "Come, Minnie."

My mother hesitates, watching me with wide eyes.

"Alexei, try to understand . . ."

I open my mouth to tell her exactly how I've tried over the last two months, but my father cuts me off.

"It's no good trying to reason with him," he says. "He's obviously determined to be unreasonable."

"Ivor, can't we talk about this?"

"No, Minnie. Alexei has to learn to make the best of things." He doesn't look at me while he talks. "We have to go. Now."

My mother looks from me to him. My father opens his hand flat, waiting, asking her—in this moment—to choose. She looks down, puts her hand in his and stands.

But at the door, she turns back to me.

"Alexei, I know it's hard. But you must give it some time."

"We're late." My father practically pulls her through the door.

The sound of a small, smothered cough jolts me. I'd forgotten all about the two footmen standing by the sideboard. They witnessed the entire scene. My father could see them from where he stood, and he'd carried on as though we'd been alone.

I clear my throat self-consciously and walk out into the passage. I look up and down to make sure I'm alone, lean against the wall and cover my face with my hands. I press my fingers against my burning eyes and swallow hard. I'll never get used to this. Never.

17

I'm lost.

I'm supposed to be on a tour of the castle with Zofchak, the castle historian. I've slogged through catacombs and dungeons and tramped up endless claustrophobic flights of spiraling stairs and listened to estimates of block tonnage and how many workers were supposedly trapped inside the walls during construction. But I ducked down a dark passage while Zofchak wasn't looking. Now I'm lost.

I wander through the home of my ancestors and try to feel some connection. The upper levels are deserted, cluttered with the broken and dusty remnants of the Russian occupation: dented steel desks and chairs missing wheels or legs, ancient typewriters with the keys permanently jammed, gutted filing cabinets and empty drawers strewn about. On the third level, yellow tape barricades an entire wing, rattling with the sounds of hammers and power tools.

The scale of the place staggers me. To build it so many hundreds of years ago must have taken a huge amount of effort and determination. The men who built it, why did they do it? Out of fear or loyalty? Zofchak probably couldn't tell me. But it's there, in the details. A carved lintel, a vividly modeled face over a door. That has to be a caricature of someone. Do men create work like this out of fear? And the men and women they built it for—my ancestors—did they ever feel trapped here? Or lost?

I wander about until I stand in the doorway of a large, clean room, like a laboratory. A half-dozen men and women bend intently over canvases and frames and small pieces of furniture or textiles, wielding tiny brushes or needles. In the background, a tinny radio plays dated American pop music. I watch them until one of the women nearest the door looks up, sees me and frowns.

"Kyahk zha vram mahko pamatsk?" she asks.

"Nyen. Spetziva." I back away, but not fast enough.

Recognition dawns on the woman's face and she jumps to her feet.

"Zhto du kavrolovich!"

I turn and run. I know I should stay, say something complimentary about the work they're doing to preserve Rovenia's heritage, but I can't flip that good prince switch the way Sophy thinks I should. It's too embarrassing to watch someone go from irritation to pudding right in front of me because of who I am.

I run along the corridor and down a broad staircase to a large open hall, supported by huge columns of pink stone, polished until it shines like glass. I skid to a stop on the marble floor, conscious of many pairs of eyes on me.

I look round, but the vast hall is empty. Only portraits, dozens of them, covering almost every inch of wall space, some hung so high they're obscured by a sort of haze.

I walk along, looking at the painted faces, my footsteps the only sound. The ancestors—the ghosts who ought to have been following me through the castle—are trapped here in oil and tempera, framed and hung on the walls.

I recognize most of the names on the brass nameplates from my grandfather's stories and deBatz's lessons, but I still don't feel a connection. There's the first Alexander, squashed and rumpled on a warped wooden panel, a beady-eyed, bearded man looking savagely out of the rough frame. Below him is the first Ivor, who I think was murdered by a cousin. I'm staring at a princess in a dress cut so low you can almost see her nipples when I hear a voice behind me.

"See something you like?"

I turn to find Sophy sitting on the last step. I haven't seen her since we arrived. She has rooms with her mother in the outer wall across the courtyard, not in the castle proper.

"Hello!" I cross the hall and stand over her. "What are you doing here?"

"The Bat is waiting for you," she says. "That historian guy is having a breakdown. He thinks you fell down a hidden passage and are lying unconscious in a pool of blood. He wants to call out a search party. But the Bat figured you were just being your usual charming self, hiding out somewhere to avoid another lesson."

"Let him wait." I sit next to her and prop my arms on my knees. It's strange, speaking English again. But not as strange as hearing Rovenian spoken everywhere by everyone. "I've heard all I want to hear on the role of modern royalty."

"Yeah? Like what?"

"Oh, all the things he thinks being royal means." I lean back with my elbows on the next step. "How royalty should exemplify the majesty of the ordinary man. Royalty must not exhibit the impulses accepted as the essence of personality in the average person. That sort of rubbish."

"You mean that royalty can't just walk away from a personal tour of the castle because they're bored?"

She smiles at me, and I kick the side of her foot.

"Ouch!" she says. "What about how royalty should never kick ordinary peasant girls?"

"I don't remember that one. What do you think of the castle? I told you it wasn't like a fairy tale. It's cold and it smells and there aren't any showers."

"We've got one."

"You're kidding! I was told it was too expensive to put one in."

"I think our rooms were furnished for the Communist administrator." She chews on the side of her fingernail. "The privileges of rank even under Communism."

She wiggles her eyebrows at me. "You can come and use it if you want."

"Huh," I grunt. "I can imagine the headlines if that gets out."

"Well, the offer stands." Sophy gets up and jams her hands into the back pockets of her jeans. "So who are all these people?"

"Varenhoffs."

She follows my path along the edge of the hall, staring at the paintings.

"Not much of a family resemblance," I say, as she examines the first Alexander.

"Lucky for you," she says. "These are some scary-looking guys. Very tough."

"You had to be tough to hold on to these mountains five hundred years ago."

"I guess." She moves on, down the centuries, stopping in front of a nineteenth-century portrait of Prince Beda, dressed in the uniform of the Upland Guards. "Now, he looks a little bit like your dad."

"He'd like that," I say. "Beda was some kind of war hero, the Rovenian Patton."

"Oh yeah?" Sophy looks at me over her shoulder. "Was your dad a soldier?"

"He was in the British army. But my grandfather made him resign his commission when Rovenia won its independence from the Soviet Union."

"What for?"

"I guess he didn't want to risk having his heir blown up or something when it looked like the restoration was just around the corner." I shift on the hard stair. "After that, when the restoration didn't happen, my dad got into horses and skiing and things like that."

"Force and industry," Sophy says, turning back to Beda. "What?"

"I was just thinking of something the Bat said. It must be rough being brought up to be a griffin and then—y'know—not getting a chance to use all that."

I hadn't thought of that. I remember my father saying how he didn't want me to have to grow up the way he did. But which was the bigger mistake, considering the way things turned out?

"It's an awful lot, Alex."

"An awful lot of what?"

"Of stuff. All of—" Sophy motions with her hand. "All of this. I didn't really get it until we got here, and I watched on TV how the people cheered and cried for you and your parents. And then this castle, and all these . . . Varenhoffs. Most people can't look back over five hundred years of people who came before them, see them and know their names and how they lived and how they died and know that it's all come down to them. It's awesome, Alex. It would freak me out."

I can't see her freaking out over anything. I can see her taking a calm look at the situation and finding a way to deal with it that she can live with.

"I think you'd do all right."

"I don't know." She comes and sits next to me. "I know you think this is nuts, but I think most people would like to give it a shot." She turns and smiles—that pretty smile. "But watching you . . . I don't know." Her smile fades. "I don't envy you, Alex."

I nudge her knee with mine and say, "Is this supposed to make me feel better?"

She grins. "Nope. But it's a perspective-maker for me."

"Glad I could help."

We're quiet for a moment, side by side on the steps.

"Most people don't really know," I say, more to the portraits than to her. "I didn't."

"Know what?"

I shrug. "The reality. Like why people are so interested. I don't understand that. Why girls scream at me. Why people want to read all that rubbish the papers print about me. I only want to be left alone."

"That makes you all the more attractive."

"How so?"

She sits up straight and holds her fist in front of her face, a pretend microphone.

"Prince Alexei is an intensely private person and we are determined to dig out his deepest, darkest secrets."

"You see?" I rub my face with my hands. "That's the sort of nonsense I can't deal with. I don't want to be analyzed and dissected by the *Weekly World Scoop*. And why should anyone care whether I'm a private person or what kind of vegetables I eat or—"

"Boxers or briefs?"

"Ugh! Exactly."

Another little silence. She nudges me with her shoulder.

"Well? Which is it?"

I shove her back.

"I'll tell you if you tell me." She smiles. Her hair is in a ponytail, but stray wisps have fallen out round her face. She pushes them behind her ears and they slip out again.

"Why don't you let your hair down?" I'm not aware

I've said it out loud until I hear my own voice echoing in the hall.

"What?" She stops smiling and stares at me.

"It's only that you always have it tied up or braided or something."

"It's a mess." She runs her hands over it, making more bits slip out. "Always getting in the way."

"You wouldn't cut it?"

She reaches back and touches the ponytail. "I've always had it long like this."

For the first time since we met, I feel uncomfortable with her. No, not uncomfortable. But not at ease. As though I have to be careful of what I say because . . .

Because I don't want her to leave.

"I've got to go, Alex." Sophy stands and pushes her hair back again. "And you're late. The Bat will not be a happy guy."

"That'll be a switch," I mutter. "You don't really have to go."

"Yeah, I think I do."

"Why?"

She looks at me for a moment, her face soft and thoughtful. She jams her hands into her pockets again and smiles a little.

"I'll see you later."

After she's gone, I sit on the steps and stare at the Varenhoffs until they become a blur, wondering what I'm looking for.

My first public appearance. I was given the choice of accompanying my father on a tour of the Padzakil iron works or attending my mother. Going with Dad would have meant a drive into the mountains, past the confluence of the Doldav and Arel Rivers, which is supposed to be spectacular. But I'm still too angry to sit in a car with him for hours and let him see that anything about Rovenia interests me.

So here I am at the Brabinsk Assisted Living Home for the Elderly. I trip over everything and don't know what to do with my hands.

The staff risk serious injury falling over each other to

welcome us, and the smell of fresh paint nearly knocks me out. I wonder if they painted just for us. At some point, I lose my mother (last seen cradling an old man, crying all over her pink suit). But I'll always have Jiri, two steps behind me. And the director of the home, who leads me back to the kitchens, where the smell of baking overtakes the paint fumes.

In the big, scrubbed kitchen, a half dozen old women are busy cooking.

"What are they making?" Take an interest, deBatz told me.

"*Fadit burka,* Highness," the director—I can't remember her name—says. "For the holiday tomorrow."

I'd forgotten tomorrow is Tarkha Day, commemorating the day three hundred years ago when Tedor I defeated the advancing Polish army. Though what little pork pies have to do with it, I don't know.

"Have you ever eaten one, Highness?" the director asks archly.

"Yes," I say. "My grandmother used to make them. She used to cut our names into the crusts."

A swift memory, the smell of spiced pork and the heat on my face as she opened the oven to let me see my pie, the juice bubbling out through my name. I get a spear of longing for her and wonder what these women would make of her, the queen in the kitchen, rolling out the pastry and singing.

The little woman next to me, frail as a twig, holds out her knife.

"If you please, Highness."

I smile at her and take the knife. But I haven't done

this since I was six, and then it was more my grandmother than me. I try to cut the dough where it's rolled flat on the flour-covered tabletop. But it stretches and shifts and when I try to hold it, I smash it with my fingers. The old women laugh at me.

"Here, Highness. Let me." The little woman takes back her knife and with a few deft strokes, cuts my name into the crust. Then she flips it onto a filled pie, holds the pie up in one hand, trims the crust and crimps the edges. She's as fast as a machine.

"You're very good at that," I tell her.

"Many years of practice," she says. "And many grandchildren. Here." She takes a pinch of cooked filling—pork and dried apples and spices—and holds it up to me. "I am always giving them a little for tasting."

I look round the kitchen. All the women have stopped what they were doing and are watching me, smiling, waiting. I can't not eat it. I open my mouth and the little woman feeds me. It's warm and sweet and sticky. "It's very good."

"Now they are giving me a kiss," she says. "My grandchildren."

So I lean forward and kiss her cheek and she pats me. Her hand is soft and cool and smells like flour. The other women break into flour-muffled clapping and make a sound like a communal sigh. They're so pleased, so happy. My face burns with embarrassment. It was little enough to do.

Afterward, we visit the freshly painted rehearsal hall of the newly reassembled National Orchestra, where we sit through the first movement of Hrebanek's *Symphony Rovenia*, which either needs work or is way over my head. I'm sweltering in my three-piece suit, overwhelmed by paint fumes and tired of smiling. While my mother talks to the conductor and shakes hands with the principals, I turn to Jiri.

"This must be very boring for you, standing about all day."

Jiri looks at me as though he isn't quite sure what I'm talking about.

"Not at all, Highness," he says. "I get to see more of my country. In two weeks, we go to Gris, where my mother was born. I have never been there. And then, I am enjoying seeing the people made happy. I am lucky." He stares up at the stage where my mother is making the first violinist laugh. "We trained three months, hundreds of us, to try out for these jobs. I am very lucky."

"Good fortune meets the ready man halfway up the mountain."

Jiri turns to me, laughing. "Yes, Highness. The old saying."

"My grandfather used to say that all the time." I'm surprised I remembered it myself.

"He would have been King Nikolas the Third," Jiri says. "I remember when we heard that he had died. All the people in our village painted their doors blue. The Communist administrator never did figure out why." He smiles to himself.

It never occurred to me that the people of Rovenia would have mourned my grandfather or thought of him as their king. I hear my mother's voice: "In a sense, you belong to them."

"Have you been in the army long?" I ask Jiri.

"Five years, Highness." His chest expands a little with pride.

"So you fought in the revolution?"

"Yes, Highness."

His face has gone slightly remote. I wish I could ask him to stop calling me Highness, but I don't think he'd like it.

"Well, I'm glad you got this job." I look down, shift my weight. "Did you get any *fadit burka* at the elder hostel?"

He looks at me and smiles. "Yes, thank you, Highness."

I sit in the back of the car with my mother, chewing on the side of my thumb.

"Alexei, what's wrong?" she asks. "It was a lovely day, and you handled yourself beautifully."

"I don't know," I say. How can I explain how mixed up I feel? It was something Jiri said, about the people being made happy. "I think I feel useless. If I really want to help someone, I ought to find a more active way to do it than smiling and shaking hands."

"You are helping, truly. We all are. Real volunteer work would be impractical. You couldn't devote yourself to more than one or two causes. But by appearing at many different places, you call attention to the issues and will draw others to volunteer. It's a large part of our job."

"It was embarrassing."

"It's only the first day, *dranyin*!" She laughs and takes my hand, threading her fingers through mine. "Give it a little time."

It's all right for my mother. In the next two weeks, she makes a real impact, almost instantly adored. Her pictures are everywhere, her hair braided and twisted round the top of her head in the traditional Rovenian style, like the girl in the cheese ads. Never self-conscious, she holds the hands of the sick and sits on the edges of beds, cradles fevered children and embraces the lonely. Working the crowds, she crouches to take bouquets from children, smiles into their faces. People cry if she even looks at them. Women call her *makla mazht*, little mother.

My father is always controlled and in charge. I stand next to him at appearances, watching him try to guide a robot hand at a factory and laugh when he screws up, make a quick quip, have everyone laughing along with him. And I remember the man in the study back in England, hysterically beating his chest, and wonder if he ever thinks about that. If it ever occurs to him that he never should have worried. He was born for this.

But for me . . . the cameras are everywhere I go, the motorized *click-click-click* of shutters as much a part of public appearances as the paint smell. And the girls are always there, sometimes in crowds ten deep, waiting when I go in and when I come out. I'm afraid to smile because every time I change expression, they break into ear-piercing screams. It's ridiculous to be afraid, but there's a desperation to the way they cry, tear at their hair, the tendons in their hands straining as they reach for me. What they want doesn't really exist. On some level, they have to know that, but they keep screaming.

19

My first solo appearance is at the groundbreaking of a new school in Gris. Security is high because of the girls. Both Malek and Jiri accompany me, though they usually work in shifts. I feel sorry for the one who isn't going to get to sleep tonight.

My father tried to seem amused by it.

"Shall I order the Home Guard to send out a tank or two?" He laughed. "Who knows what destruction a crowd of hormonal teenage girls could wreak?"

But I could tell he was annoyed at the fact that I'm expected to draw a larger crowd than he would.

The crush barriers round the construction site are set

two deep, with what has to be every member of the Gris police force stationed along them, stern in their black uniforms. But flimsy metal and fifty police officers don't seem like much, not when the crowd seethes against the barriers as our cars pull up, the noise tremendous even in the muffled cavern of the car.

When I step out of the car and straighten up, an assault batters my eardrums, thousands of girls screaming.

"Alexei!"

The wave of sound beats against me, rising in intensity as I walk. They lean over the barriers, arms stretching, straining against policemen, a mass of hands and faces, jumbled together, like a mythical beast, undulating as I walk by.

I try to shake a few hands, but when I reach out, nearly a dozen hands grasp mine and hold on, pulling me off balance. Malek has to tear some of them away. Flowers are thrust at me, and teddy bears and cards with hearts on them.

I can barely hear what the foreman and architect try to tell me about the building going up here, and I'm hoarse from shouting my replies. Anyone who thinks it would be fantastic to have hundreds of girls screaming his name and wanting to touch him hasn't got a clue.

At some point, they must be getting as hoarse as I am, but the screaming goes on. After the official groundbreaking, where the mayor and I each dig up a spade full of dirt, I'm worn down by the weight of sound.

And then I sense something, a larger swell in the crowd. Two of the barriers fall, and girls stream through, police scrambling to stop them. Instinctively, I fling up my arms. Malek and Jiri grab my elbows and drag me toward the car. But the girls pull and grab, jostling so that I'm knocked off my feet. Only Malek and Jiri's strong grip keeps me from hitting the pavement.

Hands are everywhere, in my face, my eyes, my ears, down my collar. Someone pulls my hair so hard my head jerks backward. I let out a shout, and Malek and Jiri push harder through the crowd. We reach the car, and I dive inside, cowering on the seat. DeBatz climbs in after me and closes the door, shutting out the noise. The car pulls away.

Inside, it's dizzyingly quiet. As though the buffeting screams from all directions have been holding me upright, I slump into the seat. Nobody told me the people who are happy we're here could be as dangerous as the ones who aren't.

"You certainly have an interesting impact on the female sex," deBatz says.

I turn on him. "Don't laugh about it! It isn't funny!" My head aches where my hair was pulled.

"I beg your pardon, Highness."

"You have to tell my father what it was like today. Tell him I can't do this."

DeBatz shrugs. "They'll calm down once the novelty wears off."

I lean my head on the seat, close my eyes and try to stop shaking.

I was supposed to go with my mother to a rose plantation today, but after yesterday, I couldn't face the crowds.

Not yet. For once, my parents listened to me, and I've been excused from the appearance. Instead I sit at the desk in my anteroom—the room outside my bedroom where the guard on night watch hangs out while I sleep—waiting for deBatz to load me down with work for the day.

By the window, Malek and Jiri play a tabletop version of *rhenyi*—the national sport—with a grape. I lean on my hand and watch them. Jiri makes a wild pass and tries to knock the grape back into play.

"Foul!" Malek says.

"Never! It was a clean shot," Jiri insists.

"You can't use your hand that way. It's the same as side-blocking on the field."

"He's right," I say. "It was foul."

"Ha!" Malek laughs. "Two to one, by royal decree. Set it up again."

Where's deBatz? It isn't like him to be late. I turn back to my desk and idly flip through a stack of pamphlets, newspaper and magazine articles someone's left there. They're all about the Tadesky Cataract—this huge expanse of wild, raging water where the Arel and Doldav Rivers meet, one of the natural wonders of Rovenia. I missed seeing it the other week because I was too angry to go along with my dad.

The articles are about plans to put a hydroelectric dam across the cataract, the pros and cons, the environmentalists pointing out the negative impact it will have, the power cooperative talking about how they need new sources of electricity, the government sponsors insisting it must be done if Rovenia is to move into the next century, the socialists wanting to know where the money will come from to build it.

Looking at a full-color photo in a tourist pamphlet, I think how terrible it would be to put a massive dam over something so beautiful.

"I'm sorry I'm late, Highness," deBatz says as he comes in.

I sit up in time to see Jiri palm the grape.

"I didn't know about this." I hold up one of the articles. "Is this really going to happen?"

"That's why I was late," deBatz says. "I wanted to get a copy of the latest parliamentary report."

He hands me a photocopy of "House Committee Proposal #4-89: Tadesky Dam Project." I flip through it, but it's all legal double-talk and engineering reports that mean nothing to me.

"Why do they have to put it there?" I ask. "I understand why it's important. But why there?"

"The studies have been under way since the Soviet era." DeBatz leans against the desk. "Given the cost of building the dam, the Tadesky Cataract offers the highest energy yield with the lowest environmental impact."

He's so impassive, his flat voice droning on as if it's unimportant as long as it means progress. I fold my arms on the desk and lean forward, still looking at the tourist pamphlet, the tremendous rush of water over the great rocks so vivid you can almost hear it, feel it rumbling. I wish I'd gone. I want to see it while it's still there. An ache—a ridiculous ache for something I've never even seen—starts in my chest.

"The dam is one of the many difficult decisions facing Rovenia today." DeBatz's voice is quiet. "Necessary progress is often jarring. We won't be able to hold on to everything we'd like."

I look at him and I think I can almost see it in his face. Does he feel it too?

"Excuse me, Highness, Count deBatz." Ms. Ketterman backs through the door with a plastic mail tray piled with letters and packages, which she drops on top of the pamphlets. "I thought this might help put yesterday's events in perspective."

"What is it?" deBatz asks.

"His Royal Highness's fan mail."

What is she talking about?

"Of course," she goes on, "there's too much for you to answer personally. The clerical staff handles that. But I thought it might help you to look at a few of them."

She pulls a letter from its envelope and holds it out to me. I stare at it without taking it. Written in a rounded, schoolgirl hand, it starts "Dear Alexei, I absolutely love you! You are hot, hot, hot!"

I knock Ms. Ketterman's hand away. "I don't want to see that!"

"But if you understood what they see in you, that you are a fantasy to them. It's all so innocent."

"It's not innocent." I stand up, nearly turning over my chair. "You weren't there yesterday. You aren't the one they tried to pull apart. What kind of fantasy is that? You don't know anything about it."

"I know enough, Highness." She straightens her shoulders. "And if you just—"

"Ms. Ketterman, if you don't mind." DeBatz takes her by the elbow and steers her to the door. "His Royal

Highness and I are in the middle of a most important lesson. It might be best if we talk about this later."

"I don't want to talk about it!" I shout. "And get those things out of here!"

"Malek." DeBatz jerks his head at the desk. Malek picks up the mail tray and follows Ms. Ketterman out. DeBatz closes the door behind them and turns, watching me with a strange expression on his face.

"I hate this." I pace a little. "I don't want to be this—this—pop star. I can't do it."

"It won't always be like this," deBatz says. "You must be patient."

I stop pacing and look at him. "If I have to do this, there ought to be a reason. Not simply to give a pack of idiot girls something to scream about."

"You know the real purpose. It will take time to show results."

I shake my head. "It's all talk. I don't believe it."

"No. I can see that." DeBatz folds his hands and presses his fingertips to his lips. "Perhaps if you saw the principle in action. Would that help?"

I shrug. "Not if it's more handshaking and empty speeches."

"I have something else in mind. Tomorrow we will have a more practical lesson."

The car turns down an alley along the side of the parliament building and stops next to a heavy steel door with NO ADMITTANCE painted on it in red letters. A security guard opens the door and, after a word with deBatz, lets us in. We walk down a dim, cool hallway to the lift and ride it to the main floor.

"Best if we keep a low profile," deBatz says. "The session is under way and most people are in the chamber."

Jiri and I follow him along a balcony overlooking the grand hall below. An enormous Rovenian flag hangs from the balcony. A broad staircase of the same tan marble as the walls and floor sweeps upward to the parliament chamber, where two soldiers stand at either side of a pair of bronze doors.

"This way," deBatz says. "There's a place where we can watch without being seen."

He leads us past the main doors, along the corridor curving round the chamber. Halfway along, a door opens and a young officer in a smart uniform steps out.

"Stefan?" he says as we pass.

"Hello, Grigori. It's good to see you." In spite of the impatience in his voice, deBatz seems almost pleased. "We are just on our way into the chamber."

Grigori raises his eyebrows. "Going to hear the king speak? Since when have you become a monarchist? You know, I heard a rumor while I was stationed out at Uzyatin that you'd taken a post with the Royal Service. But I knew Stefan deBatz would be the last person to support the restoration. I said as much—"

"If you don't mind." DeBatz cuts him off. "We are in a hurry. Good to see you."

"Yes, of course. I'm here for a week. We'll have to get together for a drink. Where are you billeted?"

"At the castle."

DeBatz starts walking again, and I follow, looking over my shoulder at Grigori, who stares after us. What did he mean? DeBatz was against the monarchy? What else does he know about deBatz? A long talk with Grigori would be a lot more interesting than sitting in on parliament. He might have some useful information.

"In here." DeBatz unlocks a door and ushers us in. "This is the King's Chamber. When this building was designed, the king still had a good deal of power in the government. Here he could monitor parliament without their knowing he was watching."

I step into a small, dark room. When my eyes adjust, I see a grille of carved wood in the wall and four chairs arranged in front of it.

"If you sit here, Highness, you will have a good view of the proceedings and should be able to hear clearly."

Through the grille, I see the circular chamber, the rotunda under the dome of the building. A balcony runs along the perimeter, with rows of seating for visitors. Overhead, the dome creates a sky of gilt plaster and white marble. Below, on the floor of the chamber, rows of red velvet chairs form semicircles, facing each other. In the center stands a wooden podium like the prisoner's bar in an English courtroom.

Every seat in the place is filled by the men and the few women of the parliament. My father stands in the podium in the center of the chamber.

DeBatz sits next to me. "He has already begun. Listen."

I sit back with my arms across my chest, ready for his basic speech of thanks and good intentions.

"—am aware that, uncrowned as yet, I have no official voice in this chamber, I thank you for this opportunity to make my personal appeal. In closing, let me say again, the legislation on which you vote today must include the proposed amendment to add the Russian population of Rovenia to this aid package. While I remember the kindness extended to my family, stranded in foreign lands, I must speak for those who have no voice in this country."

As soon as the polite applause stops, one of the men on the floor stands and shouts at my father.

"They must get jobs and pay their own way if they want to stay here!"

My father stands calmly, saying nothing.

On the opposite side of the circle, a woman stands and shouts back, "How can they get jobs if no one will hire them?"

From the other side, another man: "Let them return to Russia!" This is greeted by a combination of jeers and cheers.

"But many of them were born here," an opposing man stands and shouts. "And as such, have a right to the same as the rest of us."

The shouting continues for a few minutes, and then the prime minister steps forward and says, "May I respectfully request that you withdraw, Your Majesty?"

My father bows slightly to both sides of the chamber and steps down from the podium. More polite applause. After he's gone, the prime minister calls the vote. The legislation passes without the amendment my father had asked for.

I turn to deBatz. "What does that prove? Only what everyone already knows, that he's powerless."

"His Majesty's speech was one nearly every member of the House wanted him to make. He expressed the concern of Rovenians for the Russian population but allowed the government to make it clear that Rovenians must come first at this time. The government is the law of Rovenia. Your father is the conscience." He turns back to the grille. "Sometimes hope is all people really need."

I look at him, his profile silhouetted against the grille. Is he right? Can you rebuild a country on hope? I doubt it. But I got a little hope of my own today, listening to Grigori. He may be the key to finally getting deBatz off my back.

20

The major misconception about living in a castle is that people think it's a home. But the castle isn't just a big, fancy house where my parents and I live with a bunch of servants waiting on us hand and foot. It's an administrative center, where the business of the monarchy is handled. You can't walk about or sit wherever you like or pop into the kitchen to raid the fridge. People are everywhere—footmen, maids, secretaries, speechwriters, advisors and on and on.

My parents and I have had to develop a kind of code for heavy traffic days, like my mother's way of brushing a finger across her lips whenever she catches me rolling my eyes at something.

I try to stay out of the really hectic areas, but today I can't avoid it and hunt out Ms. Ketterman's office, an old armament room at the back of the castle. She's holding a mobile phone in one hand and rooting papers out of a drawer with another. She tucks the papers under her arm and covers the mouthpiece of the phone as I enter.

"Is there something I can do for Your Royal Highness?" she asks.

"Actually—" I look at a table in the corner where Sophy is writing. "I—uh—I wondered if I could talk to Sophy for a moment."

The real Ms. Ketterman shows through in a flash of irritation. But the quick, hard smile is back. Sophy stands and looks questioningly at her mother.

"Of course, Your Royal Highness." Ms. Ketterman rearranges some papers. "Go on, Sophy. But please remember we need to finish these forms for school today."

"All right, Mom," Sophy says, and follows me out of the office.

"I don't think your mother approves," I tell her as we walk along the sawdust paths in the kitchen garden, the only relatively private place we can find.

"Mmm." She stuffs her hands in her back pockets. "I think she's jealous. She cherished hopes that she'd be your confidante."

I try not to make a face. "What did she mean about forms for school?"

"Enrollment forms for the English school in Brabinsk."

"Is it a good school?" That's what she wanted.

She shrugs. "Supposed to be. I guess we'll find out."

"You'll find out, you mean." I kick the sawdust. "I'm stuck here with deBatz."

Sophy sighs.

"I'm sorry," I say quickly. "I don't mean to complain all the time. It's only . . . how am I supposed to make any friends or really get to know any Rovenians if I can't go to a normal school?"

"Did you say that to your parents?"

"They said I can go to university when I'm eighteen. Until then, they'll 'see what they can do' about friends."

"Oooooohhh," Sophy says.

"Exactly."

"Well, I'm not much, but—y'know—I'm here and all if you need me."

I reach out and touch her fingers. "I know. I'm bloody lucky to have you."

She smiles, her cheeks going pink. "And look, once school starts in September, I'll see what *I* can do about finding you some friends, 'kay?"

"That would be . . . great." I have to laugh because it sounds so pathetic, poor lonely prince. I wonder what my mates from Redfield are up to.

"So how'd the parliament thing go?" Sophy asks. "I'd love to see it."

"It was interesting. But listen. I wonder if you'd do something for me."

She cocks her head to one side. "Depends. Might cost you."

I frown. "I don't get an allowance."

"You can owe me. What do you want, Alex?"

I pull her down next to me on a wooden bench among

131

the lettuces. "I'm looking for some information about de-Batz." I tell her about deBatz and Grigori.

"You think he's like a spy or something?"

"No! I only want to know why he's doing this, if he's against the monarchy."

"How am I supposed to find out?"

"You could ask your mother. She might know. Or she could find out."

"Why don't you ask her?" Sophy hooks her elbows over the back of the bench. "Lord, she'd die of joy if you asked her for a secret favor."

"Exactly why I can't ask her."

"She'll think it's weird if I ask her."

I shrug again. "Tell her you've got a crush on him."

"Oh, come on!" She backhands me in the chest.

"Ow!" I clutch my chest. "I'm not supposed to kick you, but you can hit me?"

"It's called noblesse oblige. I think."

"So will you do it?"

She shakes bits of hair out of her face. "What? Hit you again?"

"No! See what you can find out about deBatz?"

"Why do you want to know?"

I can't tell her that I need hard evidence of wrongdoing to get him fired. Sophy doesn't know what he's really like, either. She doesn't understand that this is war.

"Because I think he doesn't want me to know."

"That's kind of childish, Al." She presses her lips together, then sighs. "All right, I'll do it," she says. "For you."

The next few days are so full of preparations for the coronation, I don't have time to think about what I asked Sophy. Inside the castle, the bustle is so great, I can't concentrate on the genealogy chart deBatz has me working on. So I take the books out to the ruined chapel.

It was irritating at first, tracing all the connections to Hohenzollerns, Habsburgs and Saxe-Coburg-Gothas. But I found out how Ulf Vrenitzi was related to me. His mother was the granddaughter of my great-grandfather's brother, who didn't make it out of Rovenia before the Soviets took over.

"You know it's impossible to get you alone? There's always someone around."

I look up to see Sophy standing in the doorway of the chapel. "Tell me about it."

"I have that information you're looking for."

"Sophy, that's marvelous!" I want to hug her but stop myself.

"Don't get excited." She sits on a lichen-covered lintel. "It's not what you think."

I sit next to her. "What, then?"

"He was hired as a concession to the opposition party. They wanted one of their own people on the inside, so to speak. Apparently, he's like a hero of the revolution or something. Highly decorated for honor and bravery. Led all sorts of intelligence missions. Very smart cookie."

I can't stop the little "hmpf" sound that comes out.

"Yeah, well," Sophy says, "he pretty much feels the same way. He didn't want the job. They had to bribe him to take it."

"Bribe him how?"

"They gave him the old deBatz manor and a big chunk of land, including the ruins of Castle deBatz in the Arels."

That's one hell of a bribe. And for someone who doesn't believe in monarchy, he's got a pretty strong appreciation of his own nobility.

"Your father was involved in the negotiations. He approved of the whole thing."

I look at the notebook on my knees, my name scrawled across the top in deBatz's strong hand. If my father knows and approves, then this information is useless.

"See? I told you you wouldn't like it."

"It doesn't matter. I only wondered." I gather up my books. "You going inside?"

Sophy stares at me for a moment, as though she's looking for something. I think I'm getting a little better at hiding things.

"Yeah, sure," she says, and stands up.

"Did your mother tell you all that?" I ask as we walk past a squad of stiff uniformed guards drilling in the courtyard.

She shakes her head. There's something different about her, but I can't figure out quite what.

"I didn't ask her. Zofchak told me. He's a big deBatz fan."

"Oh. Well, thanks for finding out," I tell her, and hold the courtyard door for her.

"Anytime."

She smiles at me as she passes and I realize what's different. Her hair is loose, hanging about her shoulders in ripples the color of dark honey. It's very pretty.

Sophy is a pretty girl.

But deBatz is waiting just inside, ready for our next lesson. I shoot him my dirtiest look as I pass, and he stares blandly back at me.

A week later, on the night before the coronation, my parents come to my room. It's the first time the three of us have been alone together—with no bodyguards, no footmen, no chauffeurs—since we arrived.

"We wanted a moment." My mother sits next to me on the bed. "We won't have a chance tomorrow."

We spent most of today rehearsing the ceremony over and over. I'm tired and all I want to do is go to bed. But I sit in my ridiculous silk pajamas and let my mother hug me.

"You aren't nervous, are you?" she asks.

"No." A kind of numbness is setting in, a yielding to the inevitable.

My father pulls a chair up in front of us and sits.

"It's all right to be nervous." He pats my knee. "It isn't a trivial thing we're doing tomorrow."

"No kidding." Tomorrow we pledge to serve a country for the rest of our lives.

My father breathes out slowly, his shoulders sagging. "Alexei, we understand more than you can possibly imagine what this means to you."

I choke, turn my head away. If that's true, it's worse than if they didn't understand at all.

My father leans forward and grasps my shoulders. "I wouldn't put that crown on your head tomorrow if I didn't believe it was worth the risk. And I don't mean just

135

the danger. I mean the risk of having you hate me for doing this to you."

My head jerks round and I stare at him.

"I don't hate you," I say, my voice tight.

"I'm glad to hear it." He smiles a little, one side of his mouth higher than the other, and lets me go.

"Since we've been here"—my mother brushes my hair behind my ear with her fingers—"haven't you seen one glimmer that your role has real meaning, that you make a positive impact just by your presence? Because of who you are?"

I close my eyes and see the faces of the last few weeks in a jumbled rush. Positive? Maybe, yes.

"I think so. I'm trying to see it."

"I've seen it," my father says firmly. "It's there. Do you believe me?"

I look at him and all I can think is that he sees what he wants to see. I can't answer and look down at my tangled fingers.

"All right." He sighs. "It's late and we're all tired."

My mother kisses me. "Get some sleep."

"Good night." My voice is a rough whisper.

My father stands and rests his hand on my shoulder. I feel a gentle squeeze before he walks away.

When they're gone, I sit and stare at the empty chair where my father sat. It's been a long time since we've had a laugh. Does he ever think about that? There are losses he hasn't stopped to count.

21

"**Highness? It is time** to get up."

I open my eyes a crack. It's still dark. Not even morning yet. Basric's off his nut.

"Check your watch. Go back to bed."

"It is five-thirty, Highness. We have much to do. Please get up, now."

Five-thirty? Ohhhh. . . . It's Coronation Day, and Basric already sounds as though he's on the verge of a nervous breakdown. I think of Drummer and of tearing away across an open field, no one about, only the wind and the grass underfoot. . . .

"Highness, if you please."

I let Basric wash, dry and trim my hair to that "hip" length Ms. Ketterman approves of. My breakfast comes up on a silver tray, and, wrapped in a dressing gown, I eat it without registering what it is, while deBatz reads off a list of moments when I might smile and when I should not. I listen and nod and eat.

DeBatz watches while I'm being dressed, as though something vital depends on how my trousers hang. I stand like a mannequin while Basric fusses over every component of my uniform. It's honorary, the dress uniform of a cadet in the Rovenian army. Spread out on the bed—blue coat, gold epaulets, white trousers with red stripes up the side—it looks like something a drum major would wear.

"If Your Royal Highness would be good enough to raise your arm."

I sigh and raise my arm. Buttons, snaps, zippers, buckles. Boots, belt, gloves, sword. Basric's usually deft fingers fumbling, pulling, pinching. But I hardly feel it. Finally, he hands me the cap, and I cram it on my head. Ms. Ketterman comes in and they all look at me as though they smell something bad.

"What?"

They don't answer. I look in the huge mirror on the wall. The uniform doesn't look as bad as I'd expected. Not like a drum major at all. In fact, it looks . . . well . . . rather good. The coat is cut to make my torso look like an upside-down triangle, as though I work out. It looks at least as good on me as deBatz's olive drab looks on him. Of course, I don't have all the medals and ribbons deBatz has pinned across his chest.

But the blasted hair sticks out under the cap and over

my ears and falls in thick waves past the stiff gold collar. I pull off the cap and hold it in my hand, but that's worse. I look like someone's scruffy chauffeur.

"Perhaps we could brush it back behind the ears?" Basric steps forward hesitantly.

I push his reaching hands away. "I don't care what it looks like."

"There would just be time to cut it," deBatz says as though it's nothing. "The barber will have been to see His Majesty this morning and may still be in the castle."

I stare at him and he stares back, his face its usual bland mask of courtesy.

"Shall I send for the barber, Highness?" he asks with utter calm.

He thinks he's given me time to see sense and cave in at the last minute.

"No." I turn to Basric. "I need a rubber band."

"Yes, Highness." But Basric only gives deBatz his fish-face look.

"I've got one." Ms. Ketterman pulls a rubber band off her wrist and hands it to Basric. "Or would you prefer this?" She pulls a black satin ribbon from her own hair.

"Please, just give me the rubber band." I hold out my hand.

"May I?" Basric asks. "I think I know what Your Royal Highness has in mind."

I stand while Basric brushes my hair back off my forehead and ears and clubs it into a ponytail with the rubber band. He cuts a bit of the black ribbon and sews it into place over the rubber band. From the front, it looks smooth and neat.

"Yes, perfect." I can't help grinning at Basric for helping me best deBatz this time. "Thanks."

Smiling, Basric hands me my hat, and I start downstairs.

The great hall has come to life, hung with garlands and banners and lined with servants, as it must have looked long, long ago. The scene seems to shimmer round the edges, as though it's a vision of the past, a time warp. But it's my own reality.

My parents are already there. My father wears a uniform almost identical to mine, a wide red sash and a bunch of medals across his chest. But my mother . . . she's in jewels and a long, shiny white gown glittering all over with crystal beads; I almost don't recognize her. She looks as though she's stepped out of one of the portraits.

My father's eyes flick over me. I can't read his expression. I think he lets out a breath, relieved. Was he afraid I wasn't going to show?

"You look wonderful," my mother mouths at me, smiling.

I scan the people gathered in the great hall. Where's Sophy? She isn't coming to the cathedral, but I'd hoped she'd show up here for moral support.

A loud banging sounds on the castle doors. Usually, only a small door set in one of the enormous double doors is opened, but now four footmen step forward, grasp the heavy iron door rings and strain to pull open both massive doors. A white-haired man in an odd skirted uniform encrusted with gold braid stands outside. He holds a large staff, taller than himself, which he raises and strikes three times on the stone step.

"Ivor, servant of the people, you are called upon to take your rightful place."

The striking of the staff knifes through me, and my heart hammers against my ribs. It's deadly serious, utterly real. I'm shaking so that I don't think I'll be able to move when it's time. I turn to my parents, but they're both looking ahead. My mother smiles as though she's out for a stroll, and my father bows his head gravely at the officer. They step through the doorway and down the steps.

I'm taking shuddering, gasping breaths, but I can't do anything about it. My ears start to ring and my vision blurs. I'm going to pass out, fall in a flat faint in my shiny uniform right here in the grand entry in front of every servant in the castle and cameras rolling right outside the door.

A firm hand grasps my elbow and propels me through the doorway.

"Come into the air," deBatz says.

At the top of the steps, we hesitate, and I gulp in the morning air. In spite of the white gloves and the warm day, my hands are icy cold and my knees shake.

"All right?" deBatz asks.

I nod and let deBatz steer me down the steps to the second of two carriages, my sword banging against my boots. The fairy tale is waiting to suck me in. Four white horses with plumes on their bridles, golden carriages, panoplied footmen. But I need to sit before I fall. I climb into the pumpkin and sink back in the red leather seat. DeBatz climbs in after me and shows me how to arrange the sword under my knees.

From somewhere very nearby, a blast of trumpets sounds and the carriage moves forward with a small jolt.

The horses' hooves and the iron-rimmed wheels make a clattering, ringing racket down the mountain road and through the streets of Brabinsk. The trembling in my knees and hands slows, replaced by numbness. I obey de-Batz's orders to wave.

All along the carriage route, the crowds of Rovenians stand sometimes fifty deep, frantically waving little blue-and-gold flags. Above the cheers of *"Varenjov!"* and the clatter of the carriages, the muffled *thump-thump-thump* of the news chopper hovers over us. Like a rapid heartbeat.

Images start to blur when we arrive at the Cathedral of St. Florian, where all the Varenhoffs have been crowned since Arkady in 1475. More trumpets. Climbing the steps behind my parents, the shouts of the crowd now unintelligible. No more smiling and waving. We're serious now.

At some point, deBatz disappears, and I flounder for a moment. But I'm not about to let anyone think I can't function without him. Inside the cathedral, I nearly jump out of my skin when Basric appears, as if by magic, to take my cap and fasten a cape of red velvet and ermine to my shoulders. Its weight drags on me. A prince in robes of ermine. All that's missing is the crown, and that's waiting at the end of the aisle.

Three bishops in embroidered cassocks stand before us and mutter blessings and prayers in deep rumbling voices. One of them asks, "Who seeks to enter this holy place?"

My father says, "Your servant, Ivor."

Music erupts from the vast organ in the loft above our heads, molten music, shaking the ancient stones, vibrating through the soles of my boots. Two little boys in white lace and red satin carry pots of incense down the aisle of the nave. The assembled representatives of the world's governments and Rovenian dignitaries stand and turn to witness the official restoration of the Varenhoff dynasty. I follow my parents, keeping my eyes on the edge of my father's train. As long as I can see it, I know I'm not stepping on it. That's all that matters at this point.

In the nave, I find my spot, marked by a tiny piece of blue tape deBatz has placed for me, and watch my father kneel and pledge himself to his country. The familiar cathedral seems transformed, different from Sunday mass. Swirling with sounds, lights, smells, charged by the heavy symbolism of the ceremony. DeBatz explained it all to me, but I can't remember what any of it means now.

A bishop steps forward and buckles a sword about my father's waist, withdraws it and offers it to my father. He kisses the sword and offers it back to the bishop, who places it on the altar, then returns it to my father, who passes it to the high commander of the armed forces. The same ritual takes place with the staff of government, which he surrenders to the prime minister. This part I understand. Proof that this is all a sham.

Throughout the ceremony, my father is constantly asked to reaffirm who and what he is. His reply is always the same. "Ivor, your servant."

Finally, all three bishops surround him and lower the crown onto his head. Inside, the crowd is still and silent, but from outside in the square where the ceremony is being broadcast on two large screens, we hear the muffled cheers of "Ivor! Ivor!" The newly crowned king stands and takes a smaller crown offered to him. He stands in front of my mother and holds the crown over her head as she kneels in front of him.

"Marie Alexandra, chosen consort of the house of Varenhoff, we dedicate you to the service of the people of Rovenia."

I watch my mother rise out of the gleaming white pool of her dress. The light from the windows and the candlelight catches the jewels in her crown and the thousands of tiny glass beads on her dress so that she glows, like something unearthly. It's almost hard to look at her.

My father stands in front of me, a small golden circlet set with uncut sapphires in his hands. My crown. It's the first time I've seen it. I stare at it. If we had never lost the throne—if my father had become king when Grandfather died—I would have received this crown in a separate ceremony on the day I turned thirteen. Would it have been easier to accept it then?

"Kneel," my father whispers.

I drop to my knees, my head bent, and stare at my father's boots.

"Alexei Nikolas Tibor Ivorovich Varenhoff, our son and rightful heir, you are here crowned Prince of Rovenia, to serve and to honor as long as you may live."

The band of the crown settles about my head. It's warm and heavy. My father holds out his hand to help me up. I stand and look into his face. He looks tired underneath the outlandish crown, with its purple cap and crusting of jewels. He leans forward, grabs my shoulders with both of his hands and presses his cheek against mine.

"It isn't too heavy?" he whispers.

I shake my head, too startled to speak. He releases me and turns away.

A bishop steps forward and announces, "I present to you Ivor, chosen of God!"

The music and singing ring out again, reverberating through the granite as though the stones have joined in. I follow my parents down the aisle and out into the sunshine, the crown on my head a tangible symbol of ownership. I am no longer my own. I'm pledged to the people cheering below us. Why they want me, I still don't understand.

22

I want to go to bed. I'm exhausted, and I'm glad. I want to fall asleep without thinking about the coronation or anything else. But I've got to stand here at this bloody ball and bow when someone smiles at me and pretend my feet aren't hurting and my collar isn't scratching my neck.

The monotonous swirling of the ladies' gowns is hypnotic. I wish Sophy were here, though she said she doesn't like glitz and glamour. I haven't seen her once in this long, extraordinary day and I feel a need for her, as though she's an anchor or my last link with normality. But she's up in the castle and the ball is being held in the Winter Palace in

Brabinsk, a municipal museum, open on the weekends for four *dashkas*.

On the edge of my vision, I sense someone watching me. Not one of the photographers that have been nearby all day, but a girl, frankly staring, quite close by. My first impulse is to run. Not that she isn't attractive. She's actually fairly hot. And that terrifies me down to my boots.

But it would be rude to run. It would be a headline. So I turn and look at her and know in a split second I'm not going anywhere. She's gorgeous, outrageously gorgeous, like a magazine cover girl, like a rock star, like a fairy. It sounds ridiculous, but if there were rock star fairies, they'd look like her. She's packed into a bright pink dress so tight it squashes her breasts up almost under her chin.

She catches me staring and smiles, a deep dimple forming in one cheek.

"It's a rag, I know," she says in accented English. "But Claude Rouen is going to give me an entire spring wardrobe for wearing it here."

I don't have a clue what she's talking about or who Claude Rouen is. But I want to say something to her, something brilliantly observant, to make her think I'm clever, worthy of her notice.

"Oh?"

"Umm." She nods, sips champagne from her glass. "I get an extra pair of shoes if I'm photographed with you."

When she says "you," she does something interesting with her eyebrows. I'm melting in my boots.

"Well, if you really need the shoes . . ."

She rewards me with a dazzling smile, waves to a

photographer a few feet away, sets her champagne glass on a nearby table and slips her arm round my waist.

I barely notice the camera flashes about us, I'm so keenly aware of the curve of her body pressed against me, warm and pliable, hot-pink folds of her skirt crushed about my legs. I think I smile but can't be sure. Finally, she steps back, waving at the photographers again. I stand dumb, short-circuited by her scent.

"That's all you get," she says to the photographers, and amazingly, they obey her and disappear into the crowd. She takes me by the arm and draws me back into the curtained alcove of the window.

"Thank you," she says. "That should be worth a pair of shoes and"—she pokes me in the chest—"a matching bag."

I ought to be disgusted with her, but all I want to do is look at her and listen to her. She hasn't said anything particularly brilliant, but I want to hear more. I don't want her to walk away. I can still feel the lingering warmth where she pressed against me.

"I'm glad to be of service," I say, hoping it sounds more clever than it is. She's probably used to sophisticated conversation. Desperately, I give her the one thing I have that might impress. "I—I'm Prince Alexei Varenhoff."

"I know who you are." She laughs, deep in her throat, and hits me gently with the back of her hand. "I don't think you know who I am, though." She looks at me sideways.

"Umm—" I scramble to put a name to her. But I can't pick her out of the parade of faces I've been introduced to tonight. "I'm sorry."

"Oh, don't apologize." She snatches more champagne

from a passing waiter. "I think it's kind of refreshing." She sips and smiles, looking at me through her lashes. "Maybe I won't tell you. Wouldn't that be fun? But some old busybody will tell you sooner or later. As a matter of fact, I have a nasty feeling this was all arranged."

"What was arranged?"

"Our meeting. Part of your publicity campaign. I don't usually get invited to these important dos. But I'll get some press out of it, and you are rather adorable."

I frown at my boots, my face hot. What she said might be true, but hearing her say it out loud, as though it's a joke, makes me feel that *I'm* a joke. She's only another facet of the whole nightmare. I ought to have followed my first instinct and run.

"I beg your pardon." I try to imitate deBatz at his iciest. "But I really don't know who you are."

She only laughs. Then she holds out her arms and makes a deep curtsy, her dress crinkling audibly as it touches the floor.

"Isabelle Vincennes." She straightens up. "The notorious Princess Isabelle."

So she's a rock star fairy princess.

"Dizzy Izzy?" She watches me, waiting for a sign of recognition. "Brat of the Côte de Braise? No? Well, somebody must think your image needs a little spicing up, and they think I'm the girl to do it."

That sounds like Ms. Ketterman.

"Oh well, it doesn't matter." Isabelle tips back her head and drains her glass. "Your watchdog is sure to fill you in."

"My what?"

She jerks her head toward the other side of the room. "That grim individual who can't seem to take his eyes off you." She waves her hand, dismissing deBatz. "How old are you, anyway?"

I hesitate. She's obviously older than I am, though it's hard to say how much. Anywhere between eighteen and twenty-five. I have a feeling she'll disappear if I tell her how old I am. Still, as she said, someone is bound to tell her eventually.

I sigh. "I'll be seventeen in August."

"Really?"

I can't tell if it's good or bad. She scans the crowd, sipping her champagne.

"Your father's very good-looking," she says. "Was it a love match with your mother or one of those dynastic arrangements you read about in books?"

I follow her eyes to where my father is standing in a small clutch of women, making them laugh.

"How did they meet?" she says slowly.

"He was invited to Denmark by the royal family to meet my mother's cousin. But he fell in love with my mother, who was visiting there."

Isabelle frowns. "Oh. Well."

"Your English is very good," I tell her inanely.

"My American, you mean." She laughs. "My mother's from Wisconsin. She was a swimsuit model. Met my dad on the beach in Fiji." She wraps both of her arms round my elbow. "I'm tired of this barn dance. Let's go for a walk."

Everyone seems to be politely ignoring us. Even the photographers have gone. Across the room, deBatz is talking with someone. It's the perfect opportunity to escape.

Jiri follows us to the door, but Isabelle puts him off.

"Don't worry. I'm not going to kidnap him. We won't go outside." She pulls me into the corridor. "There must be somewhere we can be alone in this mausoleum."

The corridor is empty, dimly lit, and the muffled sound of the orchestra echoes against the marble walls.

"Ugh, what a disgusting place," Isabelle says, her voice amplified in the cavernous hall. "You don't live here, do you?"

"No." I try to whisper, but my own voice bounces back at me. "We live in the castle, above the city."

"Poor you." She squeezes my bicep between her arm and her breast. "One of the advantages of no longer having a throne is that you don't have to live in the dreadful old castles. I've got a lovely apartment in Paris." She looks up at me. Even in heels, she's half a head shorter than I am. "You'll have to come visit me," she says.

I can't tell her I have no control over where and when I go anywhere.

"What's in here?"

I follow her past two impassive guards into a dark room where all the coronation gifts are on display behind velvet ropes so that the Rovenian people can walk through and view them.

Isabelle walks along tables displaying masses of gleaming silver and crystal, sparkling in the light from the street-lamps, and dismisses it all with a slight grunt.

"The same old trash they've been tossing back and forth for years. Stuff they've never had any use for. Someone gave it to them and now they're giving it to you."

But she's intrigued by a table of gifts from the firms

and manufacturers that have been granted royal license. Particularly a small gold basket full of scented soap roses. A small card proclaims, "Storg and Bluhndijz, purveyors of fine toiletries to the crown."

"Give me one," she says.

"What?" I'm not sure I heard her right.

"Give me one of those roses. I'd like to have one." She smiles up at me, batting her eyes in an exaggerated way.

I stare at her. "I can't."

"Of course you can. Just pick one up and hand it to me."

"If you want one, why don't you take one?" It seems such a silly, unimportant thing for her to ask. That makes me all the more reluctant to give in.

"I want you to give it to me. It would mean something to me."

She puts her hand on my arm and looks at me. I've never seen anyone like her. But I don't understand her or what it would mean if I gave her a piece of soap.

She sighs and walks away, frowning at me over her shoulder. "Well, if you don't *want* to give me a small token . . ."

I reach over the velvet rope, grab one of the white roses from the basket and practically run to catch up with her. She turns to me, her face expectant.

"Here." I hold the soap rose out to her.

She takes it in both hands, holds it to her face and inhales deeply, her eyes closed. "Mmmmm. It's lovely. Smell it, Alexei." She holds it out to me and I sniff it obediently. She smiles. "You see? We couldn't smell it across that old rope, now could we?"

"Is that all you wanted? To smell it?" I half reach for the rose, hoping to put it back, but she snatches it away.

"No, silly. You gave it to me!" She clutches it to her breast. "I'm going to treasure it always."

She walks to one of the enormous windows that front the palace and looks out into the square, at the line of cars along the street.

"I've got to go." She turns from the window. "It's been an interesting evening." She comes back and looks at me, as though she's trying to figure something out. She reaches up and puts her hand on my cheek. "Very interesting."

Rising on her toes, she leans toward me and presses her lips against mine. I'm aware of her perfume again, mingled with the scent of the rose. Her warmth and the soft pressure of her mouth on mine swamp my surprise. So this is what it feels like. I'm almost seventeen, the crown prince of Rovenia, and my first kiss is initiated by a strange girl I met fifteen minutes ago who asked me to steal a piece of soap for her. It doesn't matter. I lean into the kiss, returning the pressure.

Her tongue slips between my lips, cool and full of the sharp taste of the champagne she's been drinking. I reach for her, my hands sliding over the slippery fabric of her dress, trying to draw her closer.

Laughing, she breaks away, pressing her hand against her mouth. "Very interesting," she says again.

"Isabelle." I step toward her, still reaching, but she puts a hand flat on my chest, stopping me.

"I'm going to have to do something about this." She looks up at me. "Do you want to see me again?"

"Yes." I manage to not shout.

"Tell me, how do you feel about yachts?"

I can't even think what a yacht is. "I don't know. I've never been on one."

"Maybe I can change that." She pats my cheek. "I'll see you later."

She walks out, leaving me standing in the dark among the silver and crystal. I can still smell her, still feel the soft warmth of her lips and her body against mine, the strange, exotic feel of her tongue. The rest of the day, unreal and remote, is gone. I realize she's given me something in exchange for the soap rose, something to look forward to.

23

The enormous white yacht rests easily at anchor on the sparkling Mediterranean. Dazzling sunlight, a crescent of beach and rocky hillsides in the distance and lovely Isabelle in a microscopic black bikini stretched out on a towel on the foredeck.

If this was a dream, I'd stroll over and offer to spread some suntan oil on her smooth back. She'd sigh and roll over and kiss me again and this time . . .

"Having a good time?" a voice booms in my ear. Isabelle sits up and pulls a cover-up over her near-nakedness. Had she known I was watching her?

I turn to the man next to me. Costas Something-okos,

the owner of the yacht. A large, friendly type-A sort of man who looks as though he's about to have a coronary when he laughs or gets mad, both of which he does often. He's invited my parents and me to share his yacht for the weekend. The publicity machine approved highly, as it's good press to be seen with Costas, a big wheel in oil or something equally huge. But I knew the minute we stepped on deck and spotted Isabelle lounging in the saloon in a bright orange sundress who was really behind the invitation and why.

"I'm having a very nice time, thank you," I tell him, and he laughs, his neck distending, his face turning from red to purple with alarming speed.

"I know!" he gasps. "It's like looking in the window of a candy shop, eh? But you can't eat any because Mama's watching and she'll scold you for spoiling your dinner."

I can't think of anything to say to this staggering speech, so I only smile as though I think it's a rather good joke too.

Costas is still laughing, short, choked little hee hee hees.

"Mama is right," he says between chuckles. "That one will give you a bellyache. Trust me!" Hee hee hee.

Isabelle has disappeared. I wander round the deck for a while, staring at the water, thinking how nice it is not to have to worry about whether someone is taking my picture, letting my shoulders sag without deBatz telling me to stand up straight. DeBatz is back in Rovenia, and three days without him feels like a weekend pass from boot camp.

After a while I wander back into the saloon, where my mother is playing cribbage with Daisy, Costas's pretty young wife. My father has been with the captain of the yacht all day.

"Hello, darling." Smiling, my mother looks up from her cards, reaches for my hand and presses it briefly against her cheek.

I sit in a low leather chair and flip through the magazines on the table. Isabelle appears in the doorway, in the same filmy orange dress she was wearing yesterday. Today her hair falls in soft curls round her face. She smiles at me—I almost think she winks—and then walks over to my mother and crouches by her chair.

"Madam," she says with great courtesy. "Mr. Marenokos has been kind enough to offer me his speedboat and driver. I thought of going into town and wondered if you would allow His Royal Highness to accompany me. It's a lovely day for a run and he really should see the church while he's here."

My mother looks from Isabelle to me and back. Daisy leans across the table.

"Do let them go," she says. "Tevvy—our driver—is most reliable. He won't let them come to any harm. And of course, you'll send a bodyguard with them."

Of course. Four of them came with us, and Malek stands in the corner of the saloon right now.

Mum looks at me over her shoulder. "Would you like to go, Alexei?"

Her eyebrows have assumed the concerned position, and I'm stunned she's even considering it, that she isn't deferring to my father, to ask him if it's Best for Rovenia. I struggle to keep my face blank. I want to go with Isabelle in the orange dress, but I'm not so wild about the idea of going to town, opening up to the stares and the screams again.

"I don't know. All those people . . ."

Isabelle's eyes slide in my direction and back to my mother. "I think His Royal Highness will find it different here, madam. The people are quite used to seeing famous people on their streets, blasé, in fact."

"Alexei?" Mother asks.

"I don't mind," I say carefully.

Isabelle stands and turns her back to Daisy and my mother, trying not to laugh.

"Malek?" Mother calls.

"Your Majesty?" He steps out of the shadows.

"Please accompany His Royal Highness and Her Serene Highness into town and see that they return before dinner."

At least she doesn't say "Take good care of them." I stand before she thinks of it.

"Don't worry," I say to her.

She catches my hand as I pass her. "I'm not worried." But I know that isn't true. "Have a good time." She smiles as though she's giving me a present.

Her fingers slip through mine as I follow Isabelle, Malek at our heels.

Isabelle knows how to manage a situation. With very little trouble, she convinces Tevvy to wait with the car at the end of the boulevard while we walk past the posh little shops, Malek a few feet behind us. The sidewalk is crowded and most people don't even notice us. A few do and a flash of recognition—whether for Isabelle or for me, I can't tell—crosses their faces, but most don't say anything. Once, I think I hear a woman say to her companion, *"C'est le prince de Rovenie."*

Isabelle laughs. "You take it all far too seriously."

"What?" I'm not sure what she's talking about.

"All of it." She gestures vaguely. "Like that woman recognizing you. You went all frowns."

I can feel the corners of my mouth pulling down as she speaks.

"I don't like being stared at and talked about."

She catches her lower lip between her teeth and makes a "f-f-f-f-f-f" sound.

"Oh, you've got so much to learn. I forget this is so new for you." She links her arm through mine and squeezes. "There's nothing you can do now to change the fact that people are going to recognize you and want to look at you. Isn't that part of your job description?"

I watch the stack of jangling bracelets on her arm. "I never wanted this job," I say. "I want it less every day."

"What can you do? Tear yourself apart or accept your lot and have some fun."

"Fun?" She amazes me. "What kind of fun am I supposed to have, with bodyguards and valets and equerries following me about all the time and people staring and screaming and taking my picture every time I move?"

She stops and faces me. "You have to learn some tricks of the trade. Learn to make it work for you, Alexei, instead of fighting against it. Fun's the best you'll get out of this life, prince or not. Being a prince gives you—oh—a better quality of fun."

"How?"

She takes my hand. "Come. I'll show you." And she pulls me into a shop.

Inside it's cool and quiet and chic, all white pillars and swaths of gray cloth and stainless steel racks of clothing. Malek positions himself by the door. A young woman with stiffly sprayed hair and a severe black dress pounces on us.

"Izzy, I didn't know you were here! You should have called. We have something *très* fab for you in back. I asked Claude to save it because I knew you were the only one in the entire world who could pull it off."

"Martine, darling!" Isabelle lets go of my hand and they pretend to kiss each other. "I'm not looking for myself today. I want you to work some magic on my friend."

She reaches back, grabs my hand and pulls me forward. "Alexei, this is Martine Gilbert. Martine, this is Alexei."

"Of course he is," Martine says. "We're delighted to have you in our little shop, Alexei. I hope you'll feel as Izzy does that it's a place where you can be yourself."

I don't know what to say. The lack of formality throws me. In spite of the fact that I hate the titles and the rigidity, I feel suddenly lost without them. I almost feel I'm being made fun of.

Isabelle comes to my rescue. She seems to know what I'm thinking.

"We don't bother with titles here, Alexei. We're old friends, right, darling?"

"Oh yes," Martine says. "We understand each other."

She turns to Isabelle. "Let me tell Claude you're here. He's been dying to meet your friend, but of course, we thought it would be years before we had a chance at him. Leave it to you, Izzy. You're a genius. I told Claude so when we saw the picture of the two of you at the ball. And you looked marvelous in that dress!" She claps her hands and calls, "Charisse! Bring some Heidsieck for Princess Isabelle and her guest!" and disappears behind a curtain.

"What does she mean?" I ask Isabelle, but she's wandering about the room, flicking through the racks. "A chance at me? What does that mean?"

"It's part of the game, Alexei. You'll learn."

"Learn what? What did you mean about having her work her magic?"

"Relax!" She pats my shoulder and turns back to the racks. "We're only going to get you some decent clothes instead of those English prep school rags they dress you up in. Honestly, whoever chooses your clothing has no idea how to maximize your potential. Martine and Claude will know."

But I don't want new clothes, especially not clothing chosen by Martine to maximize my potential. More than that . . .

"I have no money."

"You don't need any." Isabelle continues to browse, unconcerned.

"I can't let you buy me clothing." I keep my voice low and one eye on Malek.

"I don't intend to buy you anything."

I follow her along the racks. "Then how am I supposed to pay? I can't have the bills sent to Rovenia."

Isabelle sighs and looks at me. "There won't be a bill. Don't you get it? You're a walking billboard, like me. People notice what you wear, where you go, what you do. For you to wear Claude's clothing is worth a lot to Claude. He can't buy that kind of publicity."

I stare at her, trying to take in what she's saying.

"I can't let him give me clothing!"

"Why not? It's what's known as a symbiotic relationship. It occurs all the time in nature."

"It's—it's—" It's wrong, it's disgusting. But I can't say that to Isabelle, remembering the dress at the coronation ball.

She turns round, pouting slightly. "Alexei, are you criticizing me? If I could tell those reporters to go away and leave me alone, I'd do it like that!" She snaps her fingers. "But you have to learn to live with it. And if that means that I can help someone like Claude, why, what's wrong with that?"

There are a million things wrong with it, but looking at her, I can't articulate a single one.

She walks a few steps away from me and turns slightly. "Well? Do we stay or do we go back to the yacht? It's up to you."

She's practically telling me if I don't join her in her "game," it's over. Back to the yacht, back to Rovenia.

"What will my parents say?" It's my last shred of argument.

"Do you really care?"

She pulls a wine-colored shirt of some thin silky material off the rack and holds it up against my chest.

"Oh yes," she purrs. "This is a good color for you."

She runs her hand down my chest, feeling the sheen of the fabric.

Claude dresses me in a loose white shirt made of very thin cotton with a faint pattern of lines woven all over it, baggy trousers the color of sand and a pair of brown leather sandals. I stand in front of the mirror and button up two of the undone buttons.

"Oh dear," Martine sighs.

"Shouldn't it be tucked in?" I ask. It looks sloppy.

"No, no," Claude says. He's dressed in tight black clothes, with very short pink hair and glasses with lenses the size of centimes. "Here." He rolls up my sleeves. "Now put your hands in your pockets and let your shoulders slump a little."

He's spouting treason. I've been told never to put my hands in my pockets unless I'm retrieving a handkerchief. But I do it. I'm not sure. I look so . . . so . . .

"Gorgeous," Isabelle says. "Didn't I tell you? You have potential, Alexei."

"It really does work." Claude stands back and eyes me critically, his thumb and finger pinching his chin. "Sort of a cross between Byron and Jesus."

"Halfway between a saint and a sinner," Martine chimes in.

Oh God. I'm going to puke on the pale gray carpeting. And I don't feel really dressed. Everything is so loose, so thin. I need the security of thick twill against my legs.

"Don't frown so much," Isabelle says. "You'll get a line

right here." She kisses her finger and presses it between my eyebrows.

Claude and Martine exchange a look. I want out of this shop.

"Hadn't we better go?" I turn to Malek, who stares at the ceiling. "What time is it?"

He looks at his watch. "Four o'clock, Highness."

"We've got loads of time," Isabelle says. She links her arm through mine and reaches out to squeeze Claude's and then Martine's hands. "Thank you, darlings," she coos. "You've done a wonderful job. Now I can be seen in public with him."

"A pleasure, my dear." Claude kisses her and whispers, "Lucky you."

"Alexei." Claude reaches to shake my hand and presses a small package into my palm. "A little present for you." He winks.

Out on the sidewalk, Isabelle tosses the box containing my old clothes to Malek.

"Isabelle!"

"What? He might as well make himself useful."

"Malek, I'm sorry. Do you mind?" But Malek shrugs and rolls his eyes.

"There's a lovely café on the corner," Isabelle says. "Let's go have a drink."

She sits at an outside table bang in view of the entire street and orders two Chambord martinis. I change mine to an iced coffee. Malek sits at the table next to us, the box across his knees. The buzz of conversation round us rises slightly and ebbs.

"See? I told you you'd like it here. Nobody cares who

you are as long as you look good. And you look fabulous." She leans across the table and takes my hand, her fingers encountering Claude's package. "Oh, what did Claude give you?"

"I don't know." The package is tightly wrapped in flowered rice paper. Isabelle snatches it from my palm and unwraps it messily. Bits of paper litter the table and blow across the sidewalk. Under all the paper is a small green bottle.

Isabelle seems disappointed. "Claude is so predictable."

I don't really care what Claude gave me, but I'm curious to know why Isabelle isn't impressed. "What is it?"

"It's coke," she says with a little snort. "Claude thinks he can woo you away from me with this." She holds up the bottle between her thumb and forefinger, looking at the drift of powder inside the green glass. "Hmmph. He doesn't know me very well."

"I don't want that. Throw it away."

Her eyebrows shoot up. "Are you sure?"

"Of course." Cocaine is the last thing I want.

"Well, no sense wasting it." She slips it into her purse. She leans across the table again, her breasts resting on her folded arms, and smiles at me. "I'm glad you don't want it. I like you, Alexei. I really like you. You might even be good for me."

Again, the feeling of disgust slips away, driven out by Isabelle's eyes, her smile, the scent of her hair. I wish we never had to go back to the boat or Rovenia.

Isabelle catches me outside my stateroom after dinner. It's after ten, and my parents are up in the saloon with the Marenokoses.

"Are you going to bed?" Her voice is filled with suggested meanings.

"Well . . ."

She leans against the wall by my door and laughs. "Your father was so funny tonight! I thought he was going to choke when he saw your clothes. He will choke if he insists on getting a bill from Claude. He's not exactly cheap."

"I told you I couldn't simply take these things."

"No. We'll have to be smarter. Only wear them when they're not around." She looks up at me. "When is that?"

"When is what?" What is it about her that makes it so hard to concentrate?

"When are your parents not around? Or your bodyguards or your watchdog?" She runs her finger up my arm, sliding the thin fabric of Claude's shirt up and down.

"They're always about, Isabelle. I'm never alone."

Her hand falls and the skin of my arm tingles in response.

"Hmm. We'll have to think about that." She pushes away from the wall. "Never mind. I'll come up with something. I always do. That is, of course . . ." Her eyes flick slightly back and forth as she stares into mine. ". . . if you want to see me again."

She's looking for something, and I don't know what. But while she's standing so close, there's only one thing to say.

"Yes." I'm surprised by the sound of my own voice, suddenly deep and husky.

Her hand slips up my arm, across my shoulder and round the back of my neck. This time I know what's going to happen and I think I'm ready for it, but it's still an electric shock. I grasp her head between my hands and hold on, not wanting to let her get away. But she pulls my hands away and steps back slightly, not laughing this time.

"I see." She turns one of my palms up and presses her lips against it, another shock, the ripple of electricity passing from her lips up my arm until my head is spinning. "It's no good this weekend." Her breath is warm and damp against my palm. "But I'll come up with something. Soon."

She walks away without looking back, leaving me propped against the wall. I'm not sure I can even make it into my stateroom. I might have to crawl. Soon, she said. I know enough about her now to believe she will think of something.

24

Sophy whistles at me from the library as I walk by. I haven't seen her much since the coronation, and I feel a little strange about talking to her, though I'm not sure why.

"What?" I lean against the doorframe.

"Nothing. Just wanted to see your tan." Smiling, she bends over her papers and writes a bit. "So what's it like being a jet-set playboy prince?"

"I don't know what you mean."

She puts down her pen and wiggles her eyebrows at me. "No? Nice shirt."

I'm wearing Claude Rouen's shirt, for which my father

paid five hundred and fifty Euros. I put my hand on my chest, my own skin warm through the thin fabric, and the whole day in Fréjus with Isabelle retreats in my mind. Too alien in the austere surroundings of the castle. I feel ridiculous. I wish I hadn't worn it.

"I get tired of being told what to wear." I feel myself stiffen.

"I'm sorry." Sophy gets up and walks round the table to stand in front of me. "I didn't mean to tease you. Honestly, it's a great shirt. You look really good."

She looks at me very seriously and we both laugh.

"I mean it!" Sophy says, laughing. "It's you."

"Do you think?"

She tilts her head, considers. "If you're a Riviera cabana boy."

"I don't know what I was thinking." I slump against the wall. "I suppose I got carried away." Except I know exactly what I was thinking, but I'm not telling Sophy.

"I guess you'll have to deal with a lot of stuff like that, like not knowing what you should and shouldn't accept when people want to give you things." Her eyes are very steady on mine. "Or who to trust."

I straighten, warning sirens going off.

"So what are you studying?" I change the subject.

She looks over her shoulder at her notebook. "Still working on my Rovenian," she says. "You know, I think it's so sweet that your mother calls you sunlight."

"What?" I laugh.

"*Denyin,*" she says. "That means sunlight, doesn't it?"

I double over laughing, my hands on my knees. "She calls me *dranyin,* not *denyin!*" I straighten up and wipe my eyes. "Oh, Sophy, thanks for the laugh. *Dranyin* means—oh—there really isn't an English word for it. It's like dear or darling but it—it's hard to explain. It's sort of a verbal hug."

"I beg your pardon, but there's a telephone call for Your Royal Highness."

Sophy and I both turn to see Basric in the doorway, holding a mobile phone.

"What?" Nobody's phoned me since we've been here. "Who is it?"

Basric's eyes flick toward Sophy and back to me. "Princess Isabelle Vincennes."

My head turns, drawn magnetically to look at Sophy. She looks back, still and quiet, her eyes wide.

"Will you take it in here, Highness?" Basric asks.

"Yes. All right," I say, still watching Sophy. I hold my hand out for the phone.

Sophy's shoulders droop a little; then she straightens and pushes her loose hair behind her ears.

"I'll—uh—I'll just go sharpen my pencil." She gives my sleeve a little tug as she walks past me, out of the room. She may not have understood what Basric said, but she certainly got Isabelle's name.

When she's gone, Basric makes a little bow and closes the library doors. I'm alone. I hold the phone as though it's made of glass, remembering Sophy's unspoken warning. Who to trust.

"Hello?"

"Alexei, darling, is that you? I was just about to hang up! God, it's like trying to get a call through to the pope!"

The sound of her voice sparks a prickling in my stomach, spreading up my spine and across my chest.

"Where are you?"

"I'm in Paris," she says. "Tell me, do you miss me? Do you think about me all the time?"

"I—" Am an idiot. Her voice short-circuits me from as far away as Paris. "Yes. I do. I think about you a lot."

Stupid! I smack my forehead.

"Good." Isabelle laughs, a low, delighted chuckle. "I've been thinking about you and I've been working hard. Remember, I told you I'd come up with something."

A hot flash of memory, melting in the corridor of the yacht, her lips on my hand . . .

"I remember."

"Well," she says, "guess who is the new patron of the Paris branch of the Society of Charitable Children's Hospitals?"

"Who?" I'm so focused on the sound of her voice, I don't hear what she's saying.

"Me, of course!" She makes a little growling sound. "Now, try to pay attention. This is important. What is your mother's favorite charity?"

My mother's got dozens of charities.

"The Society of Charitable Children's Hospitals?"

"Very good!" Isabelle laughs again. "And next week she's opening a new ward at the Brabinsk Children's Hospital. I thought it would be such a good idea for a few of her fellow patrons to be at her side. The Society loves the idea. Tons of publicity all around."

Silence while she waits for my reaction and I wait for

her words to penetrate the fog of longing her voice has kicked up.

"You mean you're coming here?" I finally say. "To Rovenia?"

"Yes!" She makes an impatient noise. "Along with the wife of the president of Germany and the first lady of Poland. Impeccably respectable company. And," she says triumphantly, "we're being put up at the castle. I'll be right down the hall."

"What? When?" The prickling sensation turns to fire.

"Next week!" She sighs. "You really must learn to pay better attention when I talk to you."

"But—but—" We'll never be alone. Not only my parents, but deBatz would hound us, I know.

"Leave it to me, darling Alexei." She draws a breath. "Trust me."

25

It's the fourth day of Isabelle's visit and it's obvious we're not going to be alone. Even Isabelle can't pull it off. DeBatz has been particularly sticky, at my heels whenever she's about. The only time he takes a break is when she's out with the other patrons. Today, Isabelle, my mother and the other ladies are inspecting the Brabinsk Children's Home. So deBatz loads me down with work, says he has some business to attend to and leaves.

I almost wish she hadn't come. It's too frustrating to have her so close and then watch her go off with my mother while I'm here, alone, with a stack of old books.

But there's someone else in the library, bent over a book at the other end of the long table.

"Sophy."

She looks up. Even across the room, I can see her cheeks turn red. "Oh, hi." She reaches to gather up her notebooks. "I was just studying. I'll get out of your way."

"No, don't."

Half out of her chair, she stops, looks at me.

"You don't have to go. I won't bother you. I have some work to do."

"I'd better go," she says.

"We can both work here." Why are we so uncomfortable with each other?

Sophy sits down again and bends back over her book. After a while, I actually get caught up in reading about coal extraction methods. It's quiet in the library, except for the sound of Sophy breathing at the other end of the table and the occasional creak of our chairs.

I look up, catch Sophy's eye and grin at her. It's good to be with her again. It's as though the world switches back to normal when she's around.

She smiles back at me. "Bought any new shirts lately, sunlight?"

But just then we hear footsteps in the corridor and someone stops in the doorway.

"Oh, hello!"

We both turn to see Isabelle posing, one arm extended along the doorframe. She looks amazing, not like she's been visiting orphans. Her dress! It follows every curve, a bright green outline of her body. Makes her hair glow red-gold. I realize I'm staring and almost have to shake myself to make words come out.

"Isabelle. What are you doing here? I thought you went to the orphanage."

"I had such a headache." She rubs her forehead, between her eyes. "Your mother thought I'd better come back and lie down."

She steps into the room and runs her hand along a row of books. "I thought I'd look for a book to read, but I don't suppose there's much light fiction in here." She makes her way round the room, carelessly caressing the spines of books as she goes. She passes Sophy and says, "Oh, hello. Sophy, isn't it?"

Sophy mutters "Your Serene Highness" without looking up.

Isabelle stops next to my chair. "Didn't you tell me you had the latest American thriller? Would you mind awfully lending it to me? I always find reading about suspense to be strangely relaxing."

I don't have any American books. But I'm getting better at following her lead.

"Yes, all right." I stand up.

She smiles, the sort of broad smile she makes in photographs, and wraps her arms round mine. I start for the door, but Isabelle stops and looks over her shoulder.

"I'll only borrow him for a minute, Sophy. You don't mind, do you?"

Sophy looks up, shrugs and goes back to reading her book.

As soon as we're in the hallway, Isabelle pulls my head down to hers and kisses me. Hard, quick kisses.

"I thought I'd never get you alone. What is *she* doing here?"

"Sophy?" I ask between kisses. Isabelle nods. "She lives here."

"I thought she lived in the *wall* or something."

"In one of the flats in the outer wall. But she comes here—" Isabelle cuts me off with another kiss, longer, her mouth opening, blasting thought.

"Isabelle—" I grab her arms and hold her off. "Someone will see us."

"You know, I think some air would do my headache good." She grabs my hand. "Let's go. I've got a car parked on the little road at the base of the castle. We'll just stroll out the gates like we're going for a walk."

"Isabelle, I can't." I'm not allowed to leave the castle grounds without Malek or Jiri. But I can't tell her that, as though I'm five years old. "What if my parents come home or someone comes looking for me?"

"Your parents won't be back until dinnertime." She runs her hand down my chest.

I close my eyes, shuddering under her fingers. "What about deBatz?"

"Oh, *pffft*. He's gone home. He goes there every chance he gets when he can leave you. Don't you read the magazine articles?"

"No."

"Well, you should. They're full of lots of useful information." She leans back, pulling on my hands. "Come on. We might never get a chance like this again."

I look over my shoulder at the library door, still open,

and wonder if Sophy has overheard us. Isabelle follows my glance.

"She won't say anything."

I'm not worried about what she'll say so much as what she'll think. But Isabelle reaches up and touches my cheek.

"Come with me."

"Is this your first time?"

"What?" The speed and gyrations of the little car scramble my brain.

"Ditching the guards," she says. I nod. "You've got to learn to be quicker on your feet, plan ahead, like me." She frowns, concentrates on shifting gears. "But don't worry. I'll teach you all the tricks."

"Where did you get this car?" I have to shout over the noise of the engine, gunning up the mountainside.

"On loan from a friend!" Isabelle shouts back. She pushes a button and the top of the car lifts and folds neatly away. Laughing out loud, she steps on the gas and shouts. "Eeyow! Alexei is *out*!"

I clutch the seat as the car swerves along the road. She's crazy. I'm crazy to be with her, to have run away. DeBatz will kill me when he finds out. If I get back. The tires squeal and throw up a scattering of pebbles and a cloud of dust from the verge of the road. Scenery flashes by in a green-and-tan blur, and the wind whips my hair across my eyes. I want to tell her to slow down, but when I look at her, she only laughs again.

"Relax!" she shouts. "You worry too much. Have some fun for once!"

Relax! How can I? I lean back in the deep leather seat and close my eyes, my breath catching in my chest. The speed drops as the car climbs higher into the foothills. I open my eyes. Isabelle's face is somehow softer, her hair blowing lightly round her face. She must feel me watching her because she turns and smiles. I smile back.

"Oh my God!" she says.

"What?"

"You do have teeth!"

"Of course I do."

"You'd never know it." She laughs. "The way you always go around scowling."

After a few miles, she pulls over, stopping the car with a little jolt that sends more gravel flying. She smiles at me again and smooths her wild curls down. "Come see what's in the trunk!"

She pulls out a checked blanket and a small basket with a yellow ribbon tied round it. Like props from an old movie. She drapes the blanket over her arm and hands me the basket.

"Come on." She leads the way through a stand of slender trees.

I follow her, carrying the ridiculous basket. "Do you know where we are?"

"No," she says without looking back. "Do you?"

"No, I don't. How will we find our way back?"

She shrugs. "We'll worry about that later." She stops and turns. "Why? Do you want to go back?"

She's challenging me. Giving me a simple choice again. "No."

She leads me through the woods until we're well out of sight of the car and the road.

"This is good." She spreads the blanket on the ground in a small clearing and kicks off her sandals. The air is warm and full of the sound of insects.

Through the trees, I can see the snowy peaks of the southern Arel Mountains rising against the dazzling blue sky. And down in the valley, I can just make out Brabinsk, with the castle standing sentry over it. It's a spectacular setting. And the trees—I think they're mountain ashes, the trees Rovenia was named for. I reach out to touch one, my fingers just grazing the glossy brown bark.

"It's beautiful here," I say.

"What is?" Isabelle looks round, puzzled.

"All of this." I wave my hand about. "The trees, the mountains, everything."

She rolls her eyes. "Don't tell me you're one of those nature types. The only thing a mountain is good for is skiing. And besides . . ." She takes my hand and puts my arm round her waist. "You didn't come up here to look at trees, did you?"

Her skin is warm and yielding under the stretchy material of her dress. I want to slide my hand over the curve of her hips. I am sliding it. She makes a small sound and leans against me. The mountains and trees dissolve around us, forgotten.

"Wait." She bends and grasps the hem of her dress. With one swift motion, she strips it over her head and then starts to undo the buttons of my shirt.

"Isabelle." I lean toward her, kissing her desperately, my hands reaching. I don't know what to do, but I have to touch her. She breaks away.

"Undo the clasp. It's in the front."

Of what? Her bra? My hands follow her orders without waiting for my brain to make a decision. I fumble with the clasp, hear a snapping sound as it breaks.

"It doesn't matter," she whispers, and shrugs the bit of lace over her shoulders. Her hands on the back of my head pull me down, burying my face in the soft fragrance of her skin. She falls backward, and I go with her.

26

Being with Isabelle was more amazing than I dreamed anything could be. She understands me better than anyone. The only problem is that she's gone. Back to her own life, and though she promised we'd be together again, I don't know when that will happen. And I don't have a choice about going back to my duties. The day after she leaves, I'm back on the job, taking a two-day tour of northern towns and cities with deBatz, Malek, Jiri and Basric.

It's different in the north. The land is wilder, more rugged. And the people poorer. We drive through Uzyatin, by far the poorest of the cities I've seen yet. Cheap, ugly houses with chunks out of the stucco; empty storefronts; dirty children kicking a can up the street; old men, as dry and wrinkled as mummies, sitting in front of the tobacconist, looking as though they're waiting for someone to come along and bury them. It's like watching an appeal for a third-world country from the private bubble of the relatively luxurious old Bentley. This isn't the Rovenia of the beribboned girls and snowy mountains being sold to the tourists.

We stop at a massive housing project on the outskirts of town, built by the Soviets in the late sixties. It looks as though it was made of cardboard and left out in the rain, as though a strong breeze would cause major disaster. There's no fresh paint here, no eager men and women in suits, showing off plans and improvements. No welcoming committee or screaming girls.

"What is this?" I ask deBatz. "Didn't anyone know we were coming?"

"The local police know we are here," he says. "There are plainclothes officers on duty. But I wanted you to see where I grew up, and I wanted you to see it unfiltered."

I stiffen for another sneak attack.

"You grew up here?" I ask in disbelief.

"Yes, Highness. There, in fact." He points to the middle of one of the towers. "We had two rooms on the fifth floor and shared a bathroom with four other families. When I was a boy, at least the plumbing still worked. There were plans to repair the old pipes last year." He turns his hawk eyes on me. "But the funds were diverted to restoring the castle."

I remember the first morning in the castle and how I carried on over the lack of a shower stall. Just what he wants me to remember. My ears burn.

"Ulf lived in the adjacent building." I follow his pointing finger almost involuntarily and think of Ulf living there, a prince, while we lived in obscure comfort in the old mansion in England.

"And over there . . ." He points to an empty lot where some boys are playing *rhenyi*. "Is where the state school used to stand. It was bombed—"

"Stefanye! Stefanye!" a woman calls from across the street.

DeBatz turns and a smile I wouldn't have imagined him capable of splits his face.

"Excuse me, Highness. I'll be back in a moment." He makes a sign to Malek and Jiri and sprints across the street.

Malek and Jiri close ranks about me.

"Does he think I'm going to run away?" I ask.

"No, Highness," Malek says. "But there are still many Communist sympathizers in this region. That is why there is such a large army garrison here. We shouldn't have come here like this," he adds disapprovingly.

My father is going to hear a large complaint when we get back, and not because of the Communists. I turn and watch the boys playing in the empty lot. One of them dives to intercept a wild pass and misses. The ball rolls to my feet. I bend and pick it up. It looks a hundred years old, all the white and black worn off. The boy who missed the block comes running up and stops a few yards away from me. He's maybe twelve or thirteen, thin with long arms and legs and knobby knees and wrists.

"*Zhrafsvyeti,*" I say.

He wipes his nose with the back of his hand. "*Zhra,*" he returns. "Who are you?"

"My name's Alexei. What's yours?"

"Vedni," he says. "Can I have the ball?"

I look at the dusty brown ball, spin it a little in my hands. "Fall back," I tell him. "I'll pass it to you."

He grins and runs backward. I put the ball on the ground, set my shot and kick it as hard as I can. It arcs over the lot. Vedni hoots and the other boys scramble to intercept. Vedni crooks his hand.

"Come on. We need another player."

I look over my shoulder. DeBatz is yapping away, his back to me. Malek frowns, shakes his head, but Jiri smiles.

"Go ahead," he says. "It will be all right."

I strip off my jacket and tie, toss them to him and run onto the field. I've never played real *rhenyi*, only the table-top version. But I know the basic rules. It's sort of a cross between football and rugby. The boys are all younger than me, but they're wiry and know the game better than I do, running rings around me and hooking the ball away just as I swing at it. But it feels fabulous to be doing something physical and not thinking about duty and all that rubbish.

I make a running leap for an airborne ball, catch it and hit the ground. Vedni and two other boys land on top of me. I roll them off and get up, laughing, to see deBatz standing on the broken sidewalk, watching us thought-fully. Any enjoyment I feel fizzles as if he's dumped a bucket of water over my head. If he says anything about me messing up my clothes, I'll kick him.

"Here." I toss the ball to Vedni. "Thanks for the game."

He makes a little salute and runs back to the lot.

"Find out their names," I say to deBatz as I stride past him to the car.

"I beg your pardon, Highness?"

"Find out their names and addresses, so I can send them a decent ball."

We drive southeast along the foothills of the Arel Mountains to Voder. But I can't appreciate the scenery because I'm on the alert, waiting for deBatz to drive home whatever point he was trying to make. But he doesn't say anything and sits, more relaxed than I've ever seen him, staring at the mountains. Once I catch him looking at me with what passes for a deBatz smile on his face. I'm tired of trying to figure him out.

In Voder, the mayor and city council members, flag-waving crowds, screaming girls and photographers welcome us to look over a new housing project. Smart little bungalows where the future residents are expected to put in a certain amount of the work.

But there's something odd about our welcome. The photographers and reporters have always dogged me, but they've been almost sympathetic. I've been able to pretend not to notice them or hear them, to look down or walk quickly away. Now there's an unpleasant familiarity in the way they call to me. It's hard to pin down. It isn't in what they say so much as how they say it, their voices when they call my name.

Inside one of the half-finished little houses, away from the photographers and the crowds outside, I grab deBatz and pull him aside.

"Is something going on that I don't know about?"

"I'm not sure what you mean, Highness."

"With them. The press." I jerk my head toward the empty front doorframe. "Don't tell me you don't notice it. There's something different about them today. As though there's a big joke that I haven't been let in on."

He stares hard at me for a moment, then pulls a mobile phone from his breast pocket and turns away. I can't hear what he's saying, don't know who he's talking to. But his voice rises.

"*Dhvu!*" he swears. "Yes, all right. Do what you can there. We will deal with it."

"With what?" I ask.

He turns, his face as impassive as usual, and slips the phone back into his pocket.

"There were some stories in the French tabloids this morning," he says.

"About what?"

He looks directly at me. "About you and Isabelle Vincennes and her stay here."

He doesn't have to say any more. I wonder how much he thinks he knows. And how the French papers knew . . . But I push that thought away.

"And that's why they're suddenly treating me as though I'm a rock star?"

"They are testing you, Highness. They don't really know if the stories are true or not." His laser eyes burn until I have to look away. "This is a delicate game. They are trying to get a reaction from you, so they can draw their own conclusions."

"What kind of reaction? You mean I'm supposed to go out there and deny these stories, whatever they are?"

"*Bozhk maj,* no! You are not supposed to react at all."

I stare at the open doorway, terrified of facing them, knowing what they know. Knowing that as far as they're concerned, my life is one big joke, a story they can sell. That perfect afternoon with Isabelle is being gasped at and laughed over by strangers hundreds of miles away.

"Whatever they say to you," deBatz says quietly, "the minute you show you care, you give them a clue. You give them ammunition. You let them win."

I see the gravity of it in his face, hear it in the earnestness of his voice. But I don't know how to play this game, not on this level. I feel as though I've crossed a line and wish I could go back.

"Any girl you show an interest in is bound to become front-page news," deBatz says, "but this one's already got a reputation. I knew she'd cause trouble."

"You don't know anything!" I turn on him. "It isn't her fault. It's them." I fling my arm toward the door. "And this whole lousy setup, laying out our entire lives in the newspapers as bloody entertainment!"

"Highness, lower your voice."

On the other side of the house, the city council clusters in a tight, worried knot.

"It isn't her fault," I mutter. "God, don't I have a right to some kind of private life?"

"This is not the time or place to speak of this," deBatz says. "I think we should go. I will make your excuses to our hosts, tell them you have a headache."

He leaves me and I try to get control of myself. Don't react. In that much, I know he's right. I can't let them see they're anywhere near the truth. DeBatz returns with the council, we shake hands, they make sympathetic noises and we walk outside.

The noise erupts as usual, the screaming girls laying

down the background track of "Alexei-Alexei-Alexei!" But over them, from the left, come the cries of the reporters and photographers.

"Alexei! Over here!"

"Look here, Alexei!"

"Give us a smile, Alexei! Good shot like that would pay for my kid's braces!"

This is nothing new. But I have to stay in control, so I don't react at all. I keep walking, looking straight ahead, deBatz on one side, Jiri on the other, Malek in the rear. No handshaking, no accepting flowers or the teddy bears thrust toward me.

"Give us a break, Alexei! Or are you in a hurry to get home to your French tart?"

I hesitate, almost stumble, but force myself to keep walking. I sense more than feel deBatz's hand hovering round my elbow.

"Is it true you two did it at the castle while your parents hosted a formal dinner?"

"Don't," deBatz says under his breath.

I can barely walk. My muscles are so tight, I move like a miswired robot.

"Come on, Alexei! Did you do Isabelle or not?"

I elbow deBatz out of the way.

"Zahknizh!" I turn and scream at them. *"Nid k'shorduv!"*

Pure reaction. No time for deBatz or Jiri to stop me. No time to think. I know it's a mistake as the words fly out of my mouth and the cameras click all about me.

27

"**What was I supposed** to do?"

"You don't swear at them, Alexei." My father paces back and forth behind his desk. "Not in Rovenian or English or pig Latin. Ever."

Easy for him to say. I wonder if he could have kept walking, kept his mouth shut while people shouted rude things at him about his sex life.

"Remember that you are a role model." My mother perches on the corner of my father's desk, giving the sense that she can only spare a moment, as usual. "I know you don't like that idea, but you must think about the sort of example you are setting."

Right now, I'm setting an example of someone who is fed up.

"So I'm not supposed to have any feelings?"

"I know it's hard, *dranyin*," she says. "This interest in our personal lives is an unhappy effect of a public life. We had hoped the papers would spare you until you were older, but Isabelle naturally caught their attention."

"Isabelle is—" I stop, adjust my breathing, adjust the volume of my voice. "Isabelle is my friend."

How much does my mother know? That afternoon . . . and the next evening, when Isabelle and I slipped away from the dinner, nobody knew. Nobody saw, I was sure. She can't know anything. Unless she believes the papers.

"She may not be the best choice of friend for you right now," my mother says.

"So I'm not allowed to pick my own friends?" I can't control my voice this time.

"This isn't just about what you want." My father stops pacing and stands in front of me. "Everything you do and say reflects on the government that invited us back."

"Don't tell me Rovenia's democratic system might topple because I told a stupid reporter where to go."

"You really don't get it." He waves both hands at me, as though he'd like to wrap them round my throat. "You aren't simply damaging a democratic system, you are putting yourself in danger. Why do you think you have bodyguards? Not just to protect you from teenage girls. We talked about this. There are people in this country who don't want us here!"

Abruptly, he turns away and runs both hands through his hair. He turns back, puts his hands on my shoulders and looks at me for a long moment.

"Don't give people reasons to hate you."

He looks half-mad, his eyes bright, his hair standing up where he raked it.

I kept my promise. I tried to do everything they wanted, but it isn't enough. There has to be something for me that's mine alone, that nobody else feels they have a right to see. A person, a place, just a moment to myself. Otherwise, I'm going to go mad.

Today is my seventeenth birthday. Ordinarily, there would have been a private family party, the usual dynastic relatives and—I had hoped—Isabelle. But she's now permanently off the guest list. And after an emergency meeting of the PR team, it's been decided to make a public occasion of my birthday, a desperate attempt to salvage my image by showing me involved in a bunch of wholesome youth-oriented activities.

If it doesn't rain, there'll be a concert in Galayda Park, singing, dancing, displays by boys' and girls' cadet groups. After that, I plant a tree. Then there's the presentation of a birthday gift from the people of Rovenia. Probably something highly symbolic, such as a goat or a large piece of cheese. And winding up the evening will be dinner with prizewinning students from all over Rovenia.

This feels so obvious, so cobbled together, it makes me cringe. I know what everyone's really thinking about me.

Cavorting in the park with a bunch of squeaky-clean Rovenian teenagers isn't going to change that.

It's suffocating in my rooms. I can't stand it, and when Basric is through with his pull-and-tug routine on my clothes, I escape down the back stairs and out a side door to the courtyard. I need some air, a second alone before we leave. But it's not much better outside. The heat lies over everything like a heavy blanket, the sky the color of pewter. I walk down the path, shuffling through the gravel.

"Alex!" someone stage-whispers.

I look round, see Sophy standing in a little arched doorway in the castle wall.

"Sophy, hello!" I haven't seen her in weeks, not to talk to the way we used to. And there's a twinge that it only occurs to me now, with her in front of me, how much I've missed that. I jog across the lawn to her.

"Can I talk to you?" she asks.

"Of course." I look at her, her hair carelessly pulled back, her eyes wide. "Is something wrong?"

"I don't know. I—" Her eyes flick over my face, but I don't know what she's looking for. She falls back against the wall. "I don't know what to do!"

"About what?" I'm really worried about her now. "Sophy, tell me. Do you want me to get someone? Where's your mother?"

I half step out of the doorway, but she grabs my sleeve.

"She isn't here," Sophy says. "She went into town. Alex, I have to tell you. I don't want to. I don't want to hurt you, but you have to know."

"Know what?" The muscles across my shoulders instinctively tense, on alert.

192

Sophy closes her eyes and takes a big, shuddering breath.

"Isabelle's here."

It's so unexpected, I almost laugh.

"What? Where?"

"In Brabinsk. That's where my mother went, to see her. I overheard her talking to Isabelle on the phone. Isabelle is going to try to see you today and my mother went to try to talk her out of it."

Isabelle's in Brabinsk! The longing to touch her and hold her is so strong, I almost sprint away from Sophy. As it is, I dance with impatience. The feel of the morning shifts dramatically. Isabelle is here. I'll see her. I don't know when. The day is so crowded. But she'll find a way. She always does.

"Alex, tell her you can't see her." Sophy pulls at my sleeve again. "Don't let her spoil today. It's too important."

"I don't know what you mean." I want to shake her off.

She squeezes her eyes shut again, shakes her head.

"God, I don't want to do this." She reaches into her back pocket, pulls out a folded piece of paper and holds it out to me. "This is coming out today. My mother knows the editor and he sent her an advance copy."

I stare at it, not sure I want to know.

"Please!" Her face twists as though it hurts her to hold the paper. I reach out and take it from her.

It's a prepress mock-up of *La Vox*, the filthiest European scandal sheet. The English edition. The headline says "Izzy Tells All: My Secret Affair with Alexei."

Underneath is a slightly grainy picture of Isabelle and me at the café in Fréjus. It's almost a physical blow, contracting my insides. I hold it out, wanting Sophy to take it back, wanting her to take back the thought she's put in my head.

"She sold you, Alex."

"It wasn't her," I say.

"It was."

"They made it up."

"They paid her. Alex, they paid her two hundred thousand Euros and gave her a car. A red Porsche. The car was an advance. They gave it to her months ago, before she even met you. That's how much faith they had in her and how calculated she was."

A flash of memory, the red convertible swerving and squealing up the mountain road . . . The pieces don't have to click into place. It's all there. Very clear. I have to gasp to breathe, but the air is thick as custard.

"How do you know that?"

"I listened in when my mother was on the phone with the publisher, trying to stop them from printing it."

I'm shaking now, and I don't know why. I knew what it was about all along, from the moment Isabelle first slipped her arm round me so we could be photographed together. She told me herself.

"I don't believe you." But it's only a desperate thing to say.

"I'm not sure how much my mother had to do with this." Sophy keeps talking. "I'm pretty sure it was her idea to bring Isabelle here that first time, for the coronation. I think she knew it would mean lots of publicity. I should have warned you then, but I didn't know for sure. And then I hoped you wouldn't fall for it. I hoped you were smarter—" She stops but doesn't apologize.

"But I think my mother underestimated Isabelle," she says. "It got out of hand and she couldn't control it anymore. But Isabelle knew what she was doing all along."

"Stop talking about her." I walk out onto the lawn, turn and walk back, trying to keep the air moving in my lungs. "You don't know her."

"I know she's using you and you'd rather poke your own eyes out than see it."

We stand a few feet apart, both of us breathing quickly, as though we've been chasing each other. And I know I can't stay, I can't listen to anything else she has to say.

"I'm late." I turn away from her. "I have to go."

Sophy grabs my arm. "Alex, don't give her another story to sell. Don't let her keep using you!"

I twist out of her grasp and walk away without a word. She's wrong. She must be. It's all some kind of huge, elaborate mistake. If Isabelle is here, she'll find a way to see me and she'll explain everything. She's always been honest with me. She'd tell me if she was involved in this.

I break into a run across the courtyard, round the front of the castle and collide with deBatz.

"Where have you been? We've got to be at the park by ten." He grabs my elbow and leads me to the drive where the Bentleys are waiting. "You cannot afford to be late for this, Highness." He looks at the paper I'm still clutching. "What is that?"

"Nothing." I fold it in fours and stick it in my pocket. It will have to wait. There's nothing I can do right now but go to my birthday party.

28

From nearly the first moment of the concert, when a girl of about twelve comes onto the stage, I know that this is going to be far more than the PR sham I was expecting. At first—seeing her with her hair plaited on top of her head, her white ruffled top and her red skirt with the rows and rows of ribbons—I expect pure cheese, the sort of thing that's supposed to draw tourists. And then she begins to tell the story of Dzenka Milla and the Hungry Mountain.

One of my grandmother's favorites. A bedtime story, to make you feel safe and secure in your own bed. But on the open stage in Galayda Park, under a lowering sky, it's like watching a dream come alive.

As the girl tells the story, the characters gather onto the stage and act it out around her without speaking. Their costumes are bright but simple, and their faces are painted stark white, the features drawn in with black and red and blue so that their expressions are as clear and simple as their clothes. Their movements are deliberately stiff and broad. They look like the jointed puppets, cut from bright paper, that the vendors sell in Brabinsk market. It's called *yegradt*, and it's the way stories have been acted out in Rovenia for centuries. I've heard of it, but I've never seen it.

Costumed children play the scenery, too: a forest of animated trees that comforts Dzenka when her mother casts her out and the villagers shun her, the river that bathes her and carries her away, and the Gorah, the hungry mountain who steals her and wants to keep her for his bride. When the mountain decides to eat the village, Dzenka feeds it—a little each day—with her blood. The village chief hears of her actions and wants her for his own wife. But Dzenka refuses him, saying she has become part of the mountain. The villagers never see her again, but they are reminded of her every spring, when the *carka*, little red flowers, pop out of the snow like drops of Dzenka's blood.

The applause takes me by surprise. I've forgotten where I am, that I'm being watched, that I'm part of the performance. The play is spoiled. As I clap, I shift and feel the folded paper crinkle in my pocket. It seems impossible that I could have forgotten about it and everything Sophy told me because of a stupid fairy tale.

A national youth choir takes the stage next and sings traditional folk songs. Some I know and some I've never heard. I recognize a melody my grandmother used to hum but would never sing the words to. Now for the first time, I hear the words sung in Rovenian.

"Krebda Varenjov, dazh pretnyzh glasda mil!"

Mighty Varenhoff, we pledge our loyalty. You are the land. You are the people. We honor your sacrifice. Feeling many eyes on me, I sit back in my seat and remember that it's not about me. It's about a Varenhoff from five hundred years ago. It's only a song, a legend.

Then two dozen boys in medieval costume mount the stage, pull out swords—real swords—and start dancing with them, swinging them beneath each other's feet and jumping over them.

"For more than fifty years," deBatz whispers in my ear, leaning forward, "no one was allowed to sing that song or dance that dance. It is amazing, isn't it, how it has stayed alive? The dance is very hard. You must train many years to do it well. It is supposed to prove that you are strong and skilled enough to fight with the Varenhoff."

Why wouldn't my grandmother sing the words to that song? It's not as though there were Communists in Surrey, censoring her.

"Would it kill you to smile?" deBatz growls.

It begins to rain. A few drops at first before the sky opens and water of biblical proportions floods the city. It rushes in rivers along the streets and steams on the pavements. Drenched medieval warriors, trees and beribboned girls run in all directions. DeBatz holds an umbrella over my head as we run to the car.

"Take His Royal Highness back to the castle," he tells the driver. "Then come back for me. I'm going to help sort things out here."

The car pulls away. I lean back and stare through the streaming window. In my pocket, a stiff corner of the paper cuts into my thigh. I wonder if Sophy is right, if Isabelle is here, and that now-familiar prickling sensation starts in my midsection and spreads a tingling warmth over my body.

The car sweeps up the hillside and through the castle gates and deposits me at the door. I go up to my room to change my wet clothes. Malek goes off to change his own.

Basric is waiting with a towel, all concern. The phone rings and he excuses himself and goes to answer it. I'm bent over, toweling my hair, when I see his shoes coming back across the floor.

"A phone call for Your Royal Highness." He sounds worried. "Her Serene Highness, the Princess Vincennes."

I straighten and snatch the phone from his hand.

"Isabelle?" I don't breathe or see or move, focused on waiting to hear.

"Happy birthday, darling!"

Her voice, light and easy, is like a rush of water, not like the downpour outside, but a clear, warm stream, taking away all the ugliness of the last weeks and the terrible doubts of the morning.

"Where are you? I need to see you! It's been horrible. You can't imagine." It comes out in a tumbling confusion of words and feelings.

"Hush, hush!" she says. She sighs, the slightest release of her breath into the mouthpiece, and I shiver all over. "You know you're allowed one birthday wish."

"Not me. You don't know what it's like here, not now."

"Oh, Alexei!" she says, exasperated. "Do you remember that day I had a headache and we took that lovely walk together? Wouldn't it be nice to do that again sometime?"

A lightning bolt comes through the phone. I realize what she's telling me.

"But—"

"Shhh." She cuts me off. "You're a big boy now. Time to do a little thinking for yourself." And she rings off.

I stand holding the phone, scrambling to remember her advice on guard ditching. Basric comes and takes the phone from my hand.

"If you please, Highness, it's only half an hour until the presentation, and you need to change your clothes."

I gape at him. I'd forgotten. But I need to talk with her. And we can make arrangements, meet later.

"I left something in the car," I say wildly. "I'll be right back."

"I can phone down to the chauffeur—" Basric says, but I'm already gone.

At the gate, I tell the warder that I dropped something on a walk the day before. He offers to find it for me, but I tell him I know just where it is and I won't be a moment. He opens the gate, and I'm out.

Isabelle is waiting on the road that runs behind the base of the castle wall. My mind makes the slightest note of the shield emblem on the bonnet of the car. She pushes open the door and I climb in. For a moment, we are a confusion of hands and hair and lips and wet faces. Her fingers tangle in my hair, her lips warm on mine. I'm lost to everything but the feel of her, not even sure I'm breathing.

"I can't believe you're here," I tell her between frantic kisses.

"I wouldn't miss your birthday. I don't care who thinks they're pulling the strings," she says, her lips moving over my face and along my neck. "I get so impatient with the way they treat you. Like you're a little boy. Or a doll for them to play with."

She knows. She's the only one who really understands.

"I wish you could stay," I murmur into her hair. "I have to go back in a few minutes."

"Who says?"

"It—it's my birthday."

"Precisely."

"Isabelle, I can't." My God, if I run out on this presentation and dinner . . . "I only came out to talk to you."

"Is that all?" She traces the edge of my lip with her finger.

She's driving me mad. I grab her hand.

"Please, we need to talk."

She jerks her hand away. "If you don't have time for me, I don't have time for you."

God! I turn and look at the castle looming over us, dark and wet and gray.

"It's up to you, of course," she says. "You can stay here and have dinner with two dozen of the most boring teenagers in Europe or you can come with me."

It really isn't a choice. I turn round again.

"All right."

Isabelle guns the engine. Tires squealing on the wet pavement, the little car rockets down the hillside.

29

Isabelle drives east, away from the city.

"The rain was a lucky break," she says. "I've had you staked out all morning, waiting a chance. Ugh. All that stomping around they were doing in the park. Who knew it was a rain dance?" She laughs, tossing her head and making her curls bounce.

A tiny niggle of misgiving. I don't laugh.

"Where are we going?"

"Wait and see." She smiles at me. "You'll love it."

So she had this planned. Of course she did. With no doubt she could pull it off. But wasn't that what I'd been hoping? I lean back in the seat and close my eyes, remembering that incredible day we drove up into the hills. Why doesn't it feel that way now? The delirious sense of escape, of freedom, is doused in rain and doubt. I try to push the questions away, but they keep coming.

I look at Isabelle, her beautiful face intent on the road, her long pale arms and little white hands on the steering wheel. Completely, utterly desirable. Right here beside me, mine for the taking. In exchange for what?

"I have to ask you something."

"You are so serious today," she says without shifting her eyes from the road. "I thought we were going to have some fun."

I pull the paper out of my pocket, unfold it and hold it out.

"Have you seen this?"

She glances at it. I think I see a flicker of something cross her face.

"I can't really look at it right now," she says. "What is it?"

"It's a newspaper. A tabloid. I really need you to look at it."

"Oh, Alexei!" She frowns, concentrates on downshifting. "You're not going to let yourself get caught up in those things, are you? It's a waste of mental energy."

"Please, pull over and look at it."

She sighs, still frowning. "Oh, all right." And pulls off the side of the road. "Let me see it."

I hand her the paper and she reads it, her face unchanging. She looks at me.

"Yes? So? It's just the usual garbage they print. You can't take it seriously. Nobody else does."

"You didn't have anything to do with it?"

Her eyebrows come together. "Of course not."

"It's pretty accurate, don't you think?"

"I don't know," she says evenly, her eyes on mine. "I don't really remember."

And then I know. I don't need her to tell me. It's so obvious, I want to be sick.

"You did," I say. "You sold them this story. For money. For this car."

We sit in silence, staring at each other. Isabelle's eyebrows have pushed up a ridge between them, and she breathes in short bursts.

"So what?" Her voice is suddenly deeper than I've ever heard it. "I told you from the start that this was a game. It's a game of survival for me."

"And what we did that day, in the forest, that was only part of the game?"

"Oh, grow up. What did you think it was? Love?"

I have to look away, through the windshield, the rain running down in a sheet that distorts everything.

"Oh, for . . ." She sighs noisily. "Don't tell me you're in love with me?"

I shake my head because I'm afraid to use my voice.

"Sure. Not now, anyway." Isabelle laughs a little. "So who told you? That American bitch? Or was it her loser daughter? I knew she was jealous. How pathetic, as if she had a prayer."

"Take me back," I say.

"With pleasure." She starts the engine and turns the car around. "You know, I was just about through with you, anyway. You're not worth the effort."

It doesn't matter. I keep thinking that, over and over as

Isabelle swerves wildly down the wet road toward Brabinsk. Maybe she'll kill us both.

The warder lets me in the gate with undisguised astonishment, staring as Isabelle guns her engine and squeals away. It's still raining, and I'm soaked through by the time I walk to the main door. I have to knock to be admitted and bear again the surprise on the face of the footman. DeBatz waits just inside, his face as stiff as his shoulders. The warder must have rung up from the gatehouse.

"Do you realize we had no idea where you were or what might have happened to you?" he demands, following me across the hall. "That a search party is looking for you and the Rovenian army has been placed on alert? I should have guessed you were with her. How she managed it, I don't know."

I know, but it's too humiliating to think about. I start up the stairs.

"Your parents are waiting in the study, Highness."

"Not now." I want to change my clothes, have a moment to regroup before I face anyone else.

"Yes, now," deBatz says. "And after you have seen them, you will change for dinner. You have missed the presentation of your birthday gift. You will not miss this dinner."

I sag against the stone baluster. There's no way I can face that dinner.

"I can't go," I say. "I just want to be alone. Tell them I'm sick."

"Enough of this childish behavior." His steel clamp of a hand locks round my elbow. "Long ago on the thirteenth birthday, Rovenian boys would jump through a bonfire. And if they burned themselves, they had to do it again. Higher, better. It's past time for you to jump the fire, Highness."

I twist out of his grip so hard a sharp pain shoots across my shoulder.

"I'm going to change my clothes first, Count deBatz. Then I'll go see my parents. And if you touch me again, I swear you'll have to fight me."

One side of his straight mouth tilts up slightly. "Who do you think would win?"

"Do you really want to find out? Right now?"

I turn and climb the stairs, every muscle in my back tensed for his attack. I know he's been waiting for an excuse, and now I've given it to him. But nothing happens.

Basric waits in my room, fresh clothes laid out. He silently helps me out of my wet things. His face, as he buttons my shirt and ties my shoes, is puckered, the eyebrows screwed up. He lets out a breath. I know he desperately wants to say something, but his rigid sense of propriety stops him.

"Say what you have to say!" I jerk away from his fussing hands. "Before you burst a blood vessel."

"Such a beautiful day it was going to be. It was a bad omen, the rain. I knew it when I saw those dark clouds."

"Dhvu!" The knot of my tie will not lie properly. I tear it open. Basric steps in and deftly reties it.

"Your Royal Highness did not even receive his birthday present."

That's the last thing I want to think about right now, but he goes on.

"Poor Miss Campbell worked so hard to bring it about, too. She was so excited."

"Sophy?" I push his hands away. "What does she have to do with it?"

"It was her idea. She wrote a letter to the prime minister and he arranged it." Basric gathers up my wet clothes. "There's a package on your desk, Highness. It was to be presented to you this afternoon." He nods toward the desk and leaves.

I look at the small, flat box, tied with a gold ribbon. Under the box is an envelope addressed "Alex." I open it and pull out a plain white card with a winged horse drawn on the front. Under the picture, it says, "If wishes were horses . . ." And inside, "Princes would ride. Happy Birthday from Sophy."

I pick up the box and open it. Inside, on a bed of white cotton, is a flat brass plate, about the length of my hand. Engraved on the plate is one word: *Drummer.*

I drop the box. "Basric!"

He comes back from the anteroom. "Yes, Highness?"

I hold out my hand with the plate lying across it. "What does this mean?"

He looks at my hand, then at me. "It's part of the gift. It was Miss Campbell's idea, for the Rovenian people to give to you."

"Give me what?" The brass is heavy and warm in my hand. "What gift?"

"Your father and the prime minister arranged to have your horse brought over from England at Miss

Campbell's suggestion. As a gift from the Rovenian people."

Drummer! I rub my fingers across his name.

"There was to be a presentation . . ." Basric's voice trails off and he sighs. "Such a disappointment."

Drummer is here. He's here because Sophy knew how much I wanted him and because the Rovenian people wanted to give me a present. I hadn't cared at all what they wanted to give me. Instead, I ran off with Isabelle as if she was all that mattered. If I'd known—would I have done anything differently?

"I'm sorry. I didn't know. I'm sorry," I say desperately, wishing that with those few words I could wipe away that look on Basric's face and the terrible mistake I've made. I can't stand it. I walk out of the room, down the stairs and out the back entrance, through the rain to the stables. Inside, it's dim and warm, the sharp smell of new wood tempered by the scent of a warm, living animal, snuffling in his stall.

"Drummer?" His head comes up, the white stripe on his nose showing in the low light. I unlatch the door of his newly built stall and step inside. Drummer bumps my chest with his head and snorts softly. At least someone is happy to see me. I run my hand along his side, feeling his warmth, the smooth hairs. I press my face into his mane, smelling his familiar smell.

Sophy did this for me. Sophy.

I can't believe I've been so incredibly stupid.

I straighten, pat Drummer, back out of his stall and secure the shiny new bolt. I've got a dinner to attend.

30

"Here, boy. Come up, lad."

Drummer lifts his head and looks at me with big, black, drowsy eyes, snuffles a few oats off my hand. It's so early the sun hasn't crested over the mountains yet. The air in the courtyard is pale gray with a mist from yesterday's rain and a heavy promise of heat. In the stables, it's dark and cool, pigeons rustling overhead and Drummer shuffling in his stall, standing where generations of Varenhoff chargers must have stood.

"Damn! Damn!"

I close my eyes and bend over the stall door. It could have been so different. It could have been an incredible morning, to come down and saddle him and take one of our headlong gallops. God, to ride Drummer across these hills, through the birch and ash forests. But I can't. Not only because I'm under house arrest, with Jiri standing guard at the stable door. But because . . . somehow I haven't the right. I've screwed things up.

"Alex?"

I look up and see Sophy standing in the aisle. The air between us is so full of things said and unsaid that when she takes a step toward me, I take an involuntary step backward.

"Sophy. Hey." I can't look at her. "Can you believe it? Drummer's here."

"Yes, I know." She walks down the aisle and stops beside me.

"Oh, right, of course." I want to kick myself. "I'm sorry. I'm an idiot. You did . . . the most wonderful thing anyone's ever done for me. I—" I look at her, but she's watching Drummer snuffle about in his straw. I have to say something. If I don't do it now, it will hang between us forever.

"Sophy, I wanted to say—about yesterday—"

"Alex, don't." She cuts me off. "It doesn't matter. I just came to say goodbye."

"What for?"

"Because I'm leaving." Her voice is flat and even. "This morning. I'm going home to America."

"What!" Another jolt. "Why?"

"I called my dad last week and told him I wanted to come home."

"Why?" I ask again, stupidly.

"Oh!" She closes her eyes. "I don't know. I'm lonely, Alex. I miss my dad. And then, my mother was fired last night. I don't know if you know about it. So I can't stay now anyway." She turns and looks at me at last, her face red and blotchy, as though she's been crying. "Even if I wanted to."

I try not to flinch.

"When are you leaving?" My throat tightens around the words.

"This morning," she says. "Now, actually. In a few minutes."

"My God, Sophy, I–" I what? I don't want you to go. I want you to stay. I don't have a right to want anything from you. But part of me is angry with her for walking out when everything is so bad. My tangled feelings tie up my tongue.

"Okay," Sophy says after a moment. "Well, I just wanted to say goodbye and tell you–" She looks at me, her eyes magnified by tears. "I didn't mean to hurt you, showing you that tabloid. I didn't know what else to do. I hated what they were doing to you, my mother and Isabelle."

The tears brim over and roll down her cheeks, but the thought of Isabelle is like an ice pick between my eyes. I blink hard, trying to squeeze it out.

"Don't talk about her," I croak.

"I'm sorry." Sophy swipes at her face. "It's just that they were both so wrong with their ideas about royalty. I hated to see you buy into that jet-set cliché." She clutches my arm as though I'm falling. "Alex, you could be so good for this country, if you could just see it. It's not too late to try."

I look at her, and the thought of never seeing her again

pierces me. I remember the first time I saw her, when she burst through the maze, furious and covered in scratches. Her face is so sweet, so familiar, the soft curve of her cheek. I reach to touch her. . . .

Sophy bursts into real sobs, her face crumpling, her shoulders heaving. She throws her arms round my shoulders and we hold each other.

"*Do videnja.*" She turns and runs down the aisle and out into the courtyard.

I fold my arms across the top of Drummer's stall door and bury my face in them. Drummer's warm breath blows on the back of my neck. It's going to be very lonely for him here, I think.

"Highness?" Jiri stands next to me, his eyebrows arched in concern. "The cars have come around and your father is on his way out. It's time to go."

I straighten and smooth the front of my jacket. I have to go make a speech.

When I finish my speech on the future of Rovenian industry and its dependence on the determination of the young, there isn't a sound in the auditorium of the Skejni School of Industry and Technology. And it isn't because I've mesmerized them with my oratorical skills or with inspiring statistics and real information they can use. Five hundred students look as though they've just come from the dentist. After a few embarrassing moments of silence, the school administrator steps up to the microphone.

"Are there any questions for His Royal Highness?"

They aren't going to ask me for the answers I memorized about unemployment figures or the vague hopes of joining the European Union. I look out over the audience, at my father standing in the back with the other administrators. He wasn't supposed to be here today, but he cleared his schedule to come with me, probably in hopes no one would throw things at me with him here. Now he gets to see me fail completely.

A thin, dark-haired student a few rows back stands and the administrator sighs gratefully.

"What do you know about the future of Rovenia?" the student asks. "You live in this country four months and think you can stand up there and tell us what a great future is in store for us. Why do you need to worry about the future?"

This is new. At least he isn't asking about my sex life.

"The future is the concern of all Rovenians." I fall back on the opening of the speech I just gave. "And the schools of Rovenia are the workshop of the future."

A wave of laughter ripples through the room and someone boos. It's like an oven. Sweat trickles between my shoulder blades. Where's deBatz? I shouldn't have to put up with this. I sense movement in the back of the room, but when I look, my father and his bodyguards are gone.

"You know nothing about our future," the skinny student almost spits at me. "You have it so easy."

"You think this is easy?" He doesn't know—none of them know what it's like. "I had a life, you know. Now I don't even own myself. I belong to you—you—" I reconsider the word I'm about to use.

"We don't want you!" A girl stands and shouts. "Why don't you go back where you came from?"

The auditorium fills with their voices, shouting back at me. "You're a parasite! Like all royalty! We don't need you! Go back to England!"

I hardly notice the administrator desperately calling for order or Malek and Jiri advancing menacingly behind me. All I know is I don't have to stand here and listen to this. I turn and stride off the stage, barely able to see where I'm going. Behind me, the auditorium erupts in laughter, and my whole body burns. I keep walking, down the steps and out the door.

Out in the lobby, my father, deBatz and a few school officials stand talking furiously, but I keep walking, straight past them. My father grabs my arm as I pass.

"Alexei, what are you doing?"

"I don't have to take this."

His hand tightens. "You can't walk out. Not now."

"Listen to them." We can hear the students, still laughing. "It was all garbage and they knew it."

"We'll think of something." He glances at the school officials, suddenly not a king but a desperate, clueless man. "We can't leave it like this. Not after yesterday. You can't afford any more bad press."

"What am I supposed to do?"

"You go back in there." DeBatz is quiet and firm.

"You're mad." I turn to face him. "They'll eat me alive."

"These are the people who will rebuild Rovenia, repair what the Soviets destroyed and the Communists could not fix," he says. "They are your peers, Highness. You can walk out on them now and reinforce everything they

215

believe about the indifference of the government to their lives. Or you can go back in there and listen to them."

He holds up his hand to stop my protest.

"When they have calmed down," he goes on, "they will have important things to tell you. Listen to them. Show them they matter, that their sacrifice is as great as yours. You can choose to do this now, choose to give your role meaning. This is what you have been looking for all along!"

Is it? His eyes are like lasers drilling into my brain, prodding me to move, to act. I glance at the auditorium door. The laughter has died down but it still booms in my head. How can I face them?

"Remember once I told you not to waste anger?" he says. "You are angry; they are angry. Use it to both your advantages."

I take a deep breath. "All right."

My father must have been holding his breath. He lets it out in a rush. "Tell them Prince Alexei would like another opportunity to speak with them," he says to one of the administrators.

"Don't worry," deBatz says.

He holds the door and I step back into the auditorium and up onto the stage. The students are quiet. Five hundred pairs of eyes watching me, waiting for me to speak. I haven't a clue what to say. I try to think of something impressive, something deBatz would say.

"I'm sorry." My palms are so sweaty, they slide along the sides of the podium. "I'd like to try again. But instead of me telling you things you don't want to hear, I'd like it if you'd tell me what you want for the future of Rovenia."

Some snickers, muffled snorts.

"No more royal speeches!" someone shouts.

Laughter again. Then someone else stands and shouts back, "Leave him alone. It took guts for him to come back in here."

"Filthy monarchist!"

Someone leaps across a row of chairs and a fight breaks out in the back of the auditorium. Malek and Jiri grab me and hustle me off the stage and back into the lobby.

"Get me out of here," I say to my father.

"Don't give up yet!" deBatz says. "They were starting to listen to you."

I stare at him. What more does he want from me?

"Go in there again?"

"Wait until they calm down," he says. "We'll try something else. A smaller group. With a mediator." He looks at the administrators, who all look as though they're about to be executed.

"Alexei, listen to Count deBatz," my father says. "For once, think about what you're doing."

"Listen to him, listen to them!" I shout at him. "Why doesn't anyone ever listen to me? I want to get out of here. Now."

The muscles of my father's face give way; his whole body deflates. Only for a second. Long enough to see how I've hurt him.

"All right. We'll go."

Two of the bodyguards walk outside. After a moment, we follow them, my father walking a little ahead of me, deBatz, Malek and Jiri behind me. Outside, the usual screaming girls with their flowers and stuffed animals press against the crush barriers. But mixed among them are people waving signs and shouting. A woman thrusts a newspaper at us.

"Is this a role model for our children?" She waves the paper at us and I see a headline, my name and Isabelle's. Not a tabloid this time but the Rovenian national newspaper. Not anonymous rumors, but an eyewitness account of someone who saw us along the road. "Is this what our tax money pays for?"

My father says something to her. He takes the newspaper and shakes her hand, to her astonishment, and ducks into the waiting car.

I hesitate at the open door of the car, dreading the long drive back to Brabinsk with my father. I glance at the second Bentley, waiting behind this one.

"Get in," deBatz orders.

"I'll ride in the other car." I take a step backward, bump into Malek.

"You are getting what you wanted," deBatz says. "We are leaving. Now stop acting like a spoiled brat and get in the car."

He reaches for my arm. I step away from him.

And then it hits. A bolt of lightning and flame. Crashing, splintering, tearing up everything in its path. Exploding, burning, all inside my head. Screaming of nerves mingles with screaming of people and I am falling into darkness.

31

I float in darkness. The black is a quiet, restful place, wrapping me in soft nothing, seeping into my ears and nostrils, slipping over the edge of my jaw and along my neck, pressing gently so that I can't move. Everything is black velvet, cool and dark and soft, no sound, no questions. I let it wrap me up.

Eventually, a sound comes through. A monotonous pattern of sound. A metallic scraping. *Rasp, click, whir, rasp, click, whir. Rasp.* My chest fills and rises. *Click.* And releases. *Whir.* And falls. A machine breathing. Making me breathe. The black tightens about me.

Sound again. Voices. People talking. Words

skittering over the surface of my brain like drops of mercury.

"... to reduce swelling ... another scan to determine ... impossible to predict ... extent of damage ... coma ..." Someone—my mother—crying, "Please, Sasha, please."

I reach for the darkness and it takes me away.

Clawing up through the dark, a physical effort. Not until I make it do I realize I've made a choice, that I could have stayed where I was. But something basic takes over, a survival instinct. I realize the dark is inside, not all round me, struggle to open my eyes.

I'm not floating. I'm lying in a bed. I can open my eyes. The room is unfamiliar, but the rasping of the machine is the same. Something is wrong. Something terrible has happened. To me. I can't remember.

I try to turn my head, to look about the room, but I can only turn a fraction of an inch. I can't seem to see anything very clearly. The room is dim, gray and smudged, like a charcoal sketch. A man sits in a chair by the bed, dozing. I think it's deBatz.

I try to call to him, call his name, but a horrible strangling feeling fills my throat. I'm choking. Something is jammed down my throat, something hard, filling it so that the muscles can't move. I try to swallow but I gag. I have to cough, have to swallow, but I can't. I can't breathe. I'm choking. My ears ring.

DeBatz gets up and runs to the door.

"Someone come quickly! He's choking!"

The room is full of people. Hands reach for me, but the darkness has come back. It floods every space, pushing out the noise and hands and the desperate gasping.

A voice murmurs. A man's voice. Soft, but deep and resonant, chanting. A prayer. Someone praying. It's God come for me. I struggle against the lead that's seeped into my veins. Struggle to say no to God.

It's so dark, I'm not sure if I've opened my eyes or not. Then I see him, close enough that I can make out his features. Not God, but my father, his head bent, saying a prayer. I close my eyes.

I have to swallow. I'm terrified, afraid of choking again. But I can't stop it. The muscles contract on their own and my throat bursts into flames.

"Horla balid," I croak, my voice unrecognizable. My mouth and tongue feel numb, slurring the words.

"What did he say?" someone asks in English.

I fight to open my eyes. Someone is standing over me. A woman. Wearing a white coat like a doctor. I blink, try to clear my vision, but she's still blurry.

"He said his throat hurts, Doctor." This is deBatz, standing on the other side of the bed. *"Anglisk, Vreshyniz."*

"Tell him it's from the breathing tube. It will pass." The tall woman—the doctor—lays her hand on my shoulder. "Can you ask him if he is in any pain, otherwise?"

"He understands English."

"His own language may be easier for him." She has an accent. Where am I?

"Kyahk vyj tsibah chustvyit? Spesid tvy uf bal?" deBatz asks.

"Nyen." Apart from my throat, I feel nothing. My mouth is so dry. I don't want to swallow again, but I need a drink. *"Jazhdanyv."* I struggle to form the words.

The doctor looks at deBatz, and deBatz translates. "He's thirsty." He turns to me. "Speak English, Highness," he says gently. "The doctor cannot understand you."

The doctor fills a plastic cup from a pitcher, puts a straw in the cup and holds the straw to my mouth. "Only a little."

My lips feel huge. I can barely make them close round the little straw. And my breath comes quickly, uncontrollably, so that I have no strength to draw the water through the straw. Straining, desperate, I try to take a breath and hold it. A small trickle of water rolls over my tongue and lips and down my chin. The water tastes funny.

Swallowing is agony. My screams come out as strangled moans. The doctor wipes my chin and mouth.

"I must find Their Majesties and tell them," deBatz says.

What's happened? Where are we? I want to ask. Instead, the doctor asks me.

"Do you remember what happened, Alexei?"

I shake my head, feel it move infinitesimally on the pillow. I can't remember. Don't want to. I wonder if deBatz will tell her how to address me properly. But deBatz is gone.

"What's the last thing you remember?"

I close my eyes. "Darkness."

"Before the darkness."

There's nothing before the darkness. The doctor sighs.

"Are you in any pain?"

I've already answered that. I blink again, desperately, but the blurriness doesn't clear. "Eyes," I say, my voice ragged.

"Your eyes hurt?"

"No." I have to wait, wait for the air to fill my lungs, to push out another rasping whisper. "Blurry."

"That's to be expected," the doctor says, as though it's nothing to wake up and have the world suddenly out of focus. "There should be some improvement in the next few days. We'll have an ophthalmologist look at you. Do you know where you are?"

I shake my head and look at the room again. A hospital. I'm probably in a hospital. But it's too hard to say. "Tell me."

"What, Alexei?"

"Where? What?" is all I can manage.

"Where are you?"

I nod.

"You're in a hospital in Hungary. You were airlifted here by helicopter."

"Why?" The word is barely audible, carried on a breath.

"There was no medical facility in Rovenia equipped to treat you."

"Nyen. Why?" I close my eyes, breathe, and open them again. "What happened?"

The doctor carefully puts the plastic cup on a small table and looks straight at me.

"You were shot. The bullet penetrated the skull, several inches above the right ear."

Silence while she waits and I wait for her words to make sense.

It can't be true. People die if they're shot in the head. Or they—or they end up in hospitals with machines breathing for them. But I'm breathing. And I don't feel anything. If I'd been shot in the head, I'd be in pain. I feel only a great heaviness, as though the sheet covering me is made of lead. And I can talk and think. People who are shot in the head lose everything. I want to tell her that it wasn't me who was shot. It was Ulf. I'm not even in the army. I want to tell her all this, that she's wrong. That people who get shot in the head end up as vegetables or in wheelchairs. Or dead.

Someone is at the door, in the room. My parents. My mother crying, murmuring my name over and over. She sits by the bed, holding fiercely to my right hand.

"I'll give you a moment," the doctor says, and leaves.

I watch her go, watch her dissolve, wanting desperately to call after her, but I don't know her name. I want her to come back and tell me it's not true.

But it is true. It's on my parents' faces. Nothing less than near death, a bullet to the brain. My father leans over to kiss me. He looks unkempt, as I've never seen him. He needs a shave. My mother is pale, her eyes ringed with dark circles, her cheeks thin. She lays her cheek against my hand, and I feel her tears, burning my skin. I register, with a tiny leap, that I can feel her, that her tears are warm. I close my fingers over hers and feel a returning pressure. I can move my fingers.

Relief is so strong it threatens to wipe out everything. My vision blanks for a moment. I wasn't even aware of the thought that had grown so quickly in a far corner of my mind. The fear that I felt nothing because I could not feel, could not move and never would. But now I know I can because my mother is holding my hand and I can feel her tears and squeeze her fingers. I squeeze again and she laughs.

My father pats my knee. I feel the firm pressure of his broad hand.

"You don't know, you don't know." My mother laughs and cries. "We thought we'd lost you." She cries in earnest, the tears splashing, soaking my skin.

"Minnie, don't." My father puts his arm round her. "It's over now. Alexei's awake. He's going to be all right."

"Yes, you're right." My mother sits up, wipes her eyes with a tissue. "It's only that these weeks have been so hard, never knowing from one day to the next . . ."

Weeks? What does she mean? She runs her fingers lightly over my forehead and lays her hand against the left side of my face. But it feels odd, as though I've had a shot of novocaine.

"The doctors here have taken good care of you," she says. "We were lucky the trade school was so near the military base and the helicopter could bring you here."

What did she mean by "these weeks"?

My mother looks up at my father.

"How are you feeling?" he asks. "If you have any pain, you must tell the doctor."

I realize he wants me to answer him, to say something, anything.

"Throat hurts," I croak again. "Hard to talk."

"Of course, *dranyin*. Don't try. Only rest." My mother fusses with the sheet covering my chest. "Oh, your hand is so cold!"

She takes up my left hand and rubs it between her own hands. I watch her, seeing my hand in hers, but I don't feel it. No warmth. I can't make the fingers contract. My hand no longer belongs to me. It's there, it's my hand, but I can't feel it or make it do anything.

"How are we doing?" The doctor comes back into the room. "You have a very determined son."

"Yes!" My mother beams at her. "And we're so grateful to you!"

"I can't stress enough how lucky he is," the doctor says. "Gunshot wounds, depending on the caliber and range, can create differing degrees of damage. Fortunately, His Royal Highness's injury is what we call focal, affecting only brain function in the damaged area. Closed-head injury, where the brain bounces around inside the skull, can cause more widespread damage. We can count our blessings."

Luck and blessings?

"You said you could tell more about his injury when he regained consciousness," my father says.

"It might be as well to let the diagnostics wait another day or two. The CT scan isn't conclusive."

"I would like to let my government know as soon as possible."

The doctor frowns at me. "Of course. I'll do some simple tests and write up a preliminary report. I must caution you that the results may change over the next weeks or even months. The human brain and its ability to heal are still largely a mystery to us."

"I understand," my father says.

The doctor smiles at me again, and her smile is more frightening than my mother's tears. She feels sorry for me. She knows.

She bends over and flashes a penlight in my eyes. First the left, then the right. Then the left again. And again. She lets out a long, slow breath and tucks the light into her pocket. She holds her finger in front of my nose.

"Alexei, try to follow my finger with your eyes without moving your head."

I follow her finger to the right and back across my face to the left. My right eye loses sight of it as it passes the bridge of my nose, and my left eye seems slow to follow. My mother makes a very tiny "oh" sound.

"Let's try it again."

The same thing happens. The doctor tries again with one hand covering my right eye and makes a note on her clipboard. I blink against the pain throbbing between my eyes.

She picks up my left hand, threads her fingers through mine and squeezes.

"Can you feel that?"

"No."

"Try to squeeze my hand."

I can't. I try and nothing happens.

She lays my hand gently back on my chest, a dead weight, and makes another note. I lie waiting, feeling the pressure of my arm on my chest, waiting for her to say something, to tell me it's temporary, to tell me it will get better. But she says nothing.

She walks to the foot of the bed and pulls the sheet back, baring my legs. "Can you feel this?"

I crane to see her stabbing at the toes of my left foot with a long needle.

"Do you feel that?" She looks up at me, surprised.

It's impossible that I don't feel it. I want to jerk my foot away from her. I want to get up and run from this bed and this room. But I can't. I can't even sit up. I reach my right arm toward her, stretching my fingers. But she might as well be miles away.

"Stop! Stop!"

"I'm sorry." She comes back to stand next to me. "I didn't mean to hurt you. But if you felt that, it's a very good sign."

I close my eyes again and breathe. Leave me alone.

"Let's try the arm again." The pressure lifts from my chest.

I open my eyes and swing my right arm at her, trying to hit her. But I have no strength. I barely touch her.

"Watch out." The doctor grabs my right hand.

I try to pull my hand away.

"All right, calm down."

"Alexei, stop this," my father says. "The doctor isn't going to hurt you."

"Leave me alone." I wrench my hand out of the doctor's grip. From the left side of the bed, she can't hold on.

"Hold him," the doctor says. "He'll lose the IV."

My father's two strong hands press down on my arm and shoulder, and the doctor comes round the bed and checks the tube attached to my arm. I can't move either arm now. I kick with my right leg, swinging blindly.

"Hold on to him," the doctor tells my father. She shouts out into the hallway.

My father lies across my chest, suffocating me. I gasp for air. DeBatz and an orderly come into the room and hold my arms and legs. The doctor sticks a needle into my arm. Stars spark behind my eyes and fracture into millions of pieces, disappearing one by one.

32

I have another IV and a fresh, horrifying memory of a battle-ax of a nurse catheterizing me as if it was nothing.

"Do you want something to drink?" deBatz asks.

I nod. He goes out and comes back with a cup and straw.

"It's ginger ale." He holds the straw to my mouth.

It burns my throat. And it tastes strange, like the water, like something antiseptic. I think my mouth will never lose the taste of sterilized plastic.

"What happened then?" he asks. "What upset you?"

"Nothing." I don't look at him. My voice is still slurred and rough.

"You didn't feel the needle? Is that it?"

"Go away."

"You must tell the doctor, Highness. This is not the time to fight."

"Not fighting." I want to tell him that I can't help it. That the reaction was something deep in the bones that took over. But talking takes too much effort.

"Do you want me to tell her?"

I shake my head once. I don't want anything. I don't want the pain between my eyes. I don't want the terrible feeling that half of me is dead.

"She cannot help you if you don't cooperate."

But my vision isn't so bad that I haven't seen it on her face. I doubt she can help me much. A bullet to the brain is an irrevocable thing.

"Don't care." I mouth the words. "Tell her."

He stands and hesitates. "You will be all right? You must lie quietly."

"I'll stay with him, Stefan." My mother is here.

Not now. I close my eyes and hear her pull the chair up to the bed and sit down.

"Feeling better?" Her voice is deliberately bright, like orange juice. Her fingers trace my eyebrow. "Dr. Lehrer says you can sit up tomorrow. She wants you to start moving as soon as possible. She's very hopeful that—" She stops, draws her hand away.

I open my eyes, still seeing her face and a pale outline. She knows too. There's a look on her face, like the look I saw on the doctor's. It's gone now. She's smiling.

"I have to tell you that they've cut your hair. I knew you'd be upset about it. I didn't want it to be a shock

231

when you see it. They had to, you see. I'm afraid it's very short, especially where—well, it will grow back."

The look again, her face torn, her heart breaking over me, right here. She turns away and wipes her eyes and nose with a wad of tissues.

"I'm sorry." She tries to laugh again. "This has been a terrible shock. I'm sure the doctor has a term for this." She mops at her eyes again. "A reaction to the strain of those three weeks while you were in a coma and we didn't know if you were going to live."

I swallow a bubble of acid. So that's what she had meant. That beautiful darkness was a coma. I had floated out of time there for three weeks. And I have to know, now.

"Tell me," I say.

"Tell you what, *dranyin*?"

"What happened."

Quietly, she sketches in the details. The speech at the trade school, the crowd outside, the man in the crowd waiting for his chance. How he came from miles away, arrived early so he'd be in a good position, waited for hours to destroy both our lives.

"When your father called to tell me, it was . . ." She puts her hand across her eyes. "We thought he'd killed you. We couldn't believe it. We knew there was danger, but I don't think we really believed—" She chokes a little, clears her throat. "But he was caught right away. He didn't even put up a struggle. And he's in prison now, where he can't hurt anyone else."

I don't want to hear any more. I don't want to know who he is or why he did what he's done. I have a fairly good idea why. I turn my head as far away as I can.

"And the Rovenians—they are in shock," she says. "Everyone is praying for you. There are special masses at the cathedral, prayer vigils. If you could see the candles and the flowers on the altar . . ." Her voice breaks and she squeezes my hand.

"You're here. You're alive. Everything is all right."

But it's not. Nothing is all right, and it never will be again. It becomes a running chorus in the scrambled mess of my brain.

An orderly brings a tray and sets it on a table that slides over my bed. He leaves, and my mother comes and lifts the silver lids from the plates of food.

"Dr. Lehrer thought you might want to try to eat something."

The smell of the food rises, nauseating. How long has it been since I've actually eaten something? I don't feel hungry. It may be I've forgotten what it feels like. Piles of pale mash fill the tray. Oatmeal, custard of some sort and a mashed banana.

My mother picks up a spoon and holds it out to me. "Do you want to try?"

I don't want to, really, but I'm terrified she'll try to feed me if I don't. I take the spoon, but my hand is shaking and I drop it clattering onto the tray. My mother picks it up and wipes it. I'm glad I can't read her face.

"Would you like me to help you?"

"No."

She hands me the spoon again, but I can't manage it.

The oatmeal is like lead, beyond my strength. I drop the spoon again. My mother lets out a long breath.

"Here." She holds a spoonful of lukewarm oatmeal to my lips. I wish I had the strength to knock it away, but I don't. I open my mouth. It still tastes like plastic, hard to swallow. I choke it down.

"It's all right." She wipes the tears from my face with a napkin and scoops up another spoonful of oatmeal. "It's all right."

I don't know how long it's been since I woke up. Weeks, I think, but I can't remember. I can feed myself now, though my meals are still near liquid. Talking is still an effort, forming the words. A speech therapist stops by regularly. Twice a day, a physical therapist pushes and pulls me about. And though he's had me sit on the edge of the bed, moved me to a chair and back again, I don't feel I've gained anything. But Dr. Lehrer seems pleased.

"You may still see a great deal of improvement over time," she tells my parents, talking over me as though I'm not even there. "The facial paralysis is improving already, and the speech issues with it. But there really is little more we can do for His Royal Highness here," she admits. "I recommend a rehabilitation facility to help him learn to deal with his disability."

"Don't call it that," I snap at her.

"Alexei." My mother talks to me as she always does now, as though I'm a small child. "Dr. Lehrer is trying to help you."

"It's all right," Dr. Lehrer says. "Quite often, the anxiety these patients feel is manifested in different ways. Rudeness, striking out are coping mechanisms."

I stare at the blank page of the ceiling. The doctor's words have bounced me onto a new conveyor belt. I am now one of "these patients," "disabled." Just being Alex is now completely beyond my reach.

"I can give you a recommendation to the very best rehab hospital, on the cutting edge in dealing with traumatic brain injury."

"If you don't mind, may I have a word?" My father motions to the door and, with my mother, follows Dr. Lehrer out of my room.

I turn to look through the glass wall, but Dr. Lehrer and my parents aren't in the hall. DeBatz leans against the doorframe.

"What's going on?" I ask.

"The arrangements for your convalescence have already been made," deBatz says. "His Majesty is explaining to the doctor."

I don't want to go to another hospital. A rehabilitation facility. An awful pair of words, like a factory, churning out people who can deal with their disabilities. But what choice do I have?

"Where—" My voice cracks idiotically.

"We return to Brabinsk next week. A private physical therapist has been hired to work with you at the castle. The idea of a rehabilitation hospital was rejected because of security risks."

In case someone wants to finish the job. I blink hard.

"I don't want to go back."

"You never did."

"They don't want me, the Rovenians. Not now—especially—" I clear my throat. "I can't go back. I don't want anyone there to see me like this."

DeBatz pushes away from the wall and stands by my bed. "They won't see you. You'll be in the castle."

But the castle is far from private. And—how can I say it? To this man who is afraid of nothing. I swallow hard and close my eyes.

"I'm afraid."

"Of what?" DeBatz's voice is level, quiet. "The man who shot you is in prison."

I shake my head so hard it aches. I don't want to think about him, don't want to know. But the questions are always there. The who and why.

"There has to be somewhere else. I can't go back yet. Not—" Not like this. But what if this is all there will ever be? "Not yet."

DeBatz stands silently, looking out into the hall. He murmurs, "Excuse me," and leaves.

Why should I expect him to help me? He's never been on my side.

"Alexei, I want to ask you a question."

My father and I haven't been alone since the night I woke and found him praying by my bed. I'm sitting up in bed, but I don't like it. Flat is safer.

"Count deBatz has suggested an alternative to taking

236

you back to Rovenia right away. I want to know how you feel about it."

"What did he say to you?" I clutch the bed rail. I can't remember what I said to deBatz yesterday. I know I told him things I wish I hadn't.

"Only that he thought you might be more comfortable if you could recuperate in a more secluded setting. He proposes a private home here in Hungary, with himself as your primary caretaker. The physical therapist has agreed to help locate and set up the equipment you'll need, as well as to train deBatz to handle the bulk of your therapy. The therapists will visit you periodically, but deBatz will work with you on a daily basis. You wouldn't have to deal with any other outsiders." He leans forward, his hand next to mine on the bed rail. "What do you think?"

DeBatz has done this thing for me? He heard me and saw what my parents didn't?

"Your mother and I would have to return to Rovenia, but we'd visit you as often as we could," my father says. "Of course, we'd rather have you with us, but you must choose what feels right for you."

Oh God. He knows that I don't want to go back to Rovenia, but I don't think he understands why.

"I can't—" I start. But there isn't any way to make him understand. I don't want to hurt him, but I don't have the strength not to.

DeBatz's alternative isn't much more attractive. In fact, it's downright terrifying. The deBatz in this hospital is not the deBatz I'm used to hating. I don't know how to react to him. The thought of living with him on these new terms isn't something I'd willingly choose. But this is what it's come down to.

"I think—" I pick my words. "Count deBatz's plan might work best. For now."

My father sits back in the chair, as though someone has given him a gentle shove.

"All right, Alexei. I'll see that the plans are made."

33

It comes again, the fire, the smoke, the searing lightning, plowing through my brain, exploding inside my skull, blasting neurons. Nerve endings scream. I want to cover my ears, get away from the noise, but I can't lift my hands.

"*Dyshka*. It's all right! Quiet, now. You're all right."

DeBatz. He wipes my forehead and pulls the blankets up over my chest. Then he helps me sit up a little and holds a cup for me to drink from. It's tea. Warm and very sweet. I lie back down and stare up at another ceiling.

But this one is different, painted in a rough representation of a summer sky, blue with great blobs of white clouds. From one corner, a flight of birds with long necks and trailing legs fans out across the sky. I turn my head. Trees and vines creep up the walls, starred with pink-and-white flowers. I blink, trying to focus. Among the leaves, I think I see a small monkey with a white face.

"Where are we?"

"About fifty miles east of Budapest. You've been asleep for almost twenty-four hours." He crosses to a tall window and pulls aside the drapes. Sunlight fills the room. I squint, shading my eyes with my hand.

I must have fallen asleep in the car, but I can't remember. That happens sometimes. I'll forget that I've eaten or can't remember something someone told me just a few minutes before. And sometimes when I wake up, I forget what happened and have to remember it all over again.

I look at the vine-covered walls. It's very quiet here. Not like the humming bustle that underlay everything at the hospital. It's a patient sort of a peace. A place to wait for things to happen. It's an ominous feeling.

"Whose house is this?" I ask, to make a dent in the quiet.

DeBatz smooths the drapes. "It belongs to the Vrenitzi family. Ulf's parents fled here the year before the revolution. After Ulf was killed."

Quiet again. The Vrenitzis' house. The monkey stares at me from the wall.

"Are they here?" I don't think I can manage a presentation right now.

"No." DeBatz fiddles with the window shade. "The grand duke died several years ago. The grand duchess lives in Venice." He turns round. "Are you hungry? Would you like something to eat?"

I'm not hungry, but I nod. If he goes, it will give me a moment to shake off the nightmare.

DeBatz picks up a phone from a table next to my bed. "Basric. Bring His Royal Highness's breakfast to his room."

I stare at the phone as though it's going to morph into Basric on the spot. "Basric? What's he doing here?" It's asking too much, to face him now.

"He asked to come." DeBatz presses a button on the bed rail and the head of the bed rises with an electrical hum.

"I don't want him here."

"I can't care for you alone." DeBatz leans across the bed and folds the sheet down about my waist. His voice is as smooth as his face. "Basric is trustworthy and, in case you hadn't noticed, devoted to you."

I wait for him to say "not that you deserve it," but it doesn't come. Why should Basric feel any sort of devotion to me? I've done nothing but treat him like a doormat from the day we met.

There's a polite knock and Basric backs through the door, a bed tray in his hands. He turns, the wide smile on his face dissolving into a tiny *o*, and nearly drops the loaded tray. Cutlery clinks against china as he scrambles to hold on to the tray.

"Good morning, Highness," he says, putting his face to rights and settling the tray across my lap. "And may I say wh-what a pleasure it is to-to—" His prepared speech dries up. He clears his throat and spreads a napkin across my chest. "A pleasure to serve you again, Highness."

I have to say something. "Thank you, Basric," I manage. But it's enough. Smiling, he backs out of the room.

I stare at toast, curried eggs and some sort of meat already cut into little pieces. If I'd had any appetite at all, it's gone now. I've just seen a reflection of myself on Basric's face. Have I changed that much? Enough to frighten Basric into dropping things? How bad is it? Is it the hair? My mother said it was very short, but I haven't wanted to touch my head, to feel it.

"You should have warned Basric."

"About what?" DeBatz looks up from some papers he's cramming into a folder.

"About the way I look. It was cruel."

DeBatz turns back to his papers. "I did warn him."

Fumbling, I find a spoon on the tray and hold it up, trying to see myself in the bowl. But it's no good. A tiny image of a pale face, distorted on the convex side, inverted on the concave.

"Would you—" I stop, clear my throat. "Would you bring me a mirror? Please?"

DeBatz straightens and looks at me for a moment. "Are you sure? It might be a good idea to wait, until your body has a chance to recover more."

I shake my head.

"Very well." He leaves. I hear footsteps going up stairs, floorboards creaking somewhere over me. I hear his distinctive cadence returning along the hall and realize I've been holding my breath. How bad can it be?

DeBatz returns and hands me a silver hand mirror. It's

heavy, and I nearly drop it in my eggs. DeBatz reaches for it, but I shake my head, tighten my grip and lift it.

But it's not my face that looks out. It's a mask of my face, a mask that has somehow melted, the left side sagging horribly. My skin is so pale the veins stand out blue, and the rings beneath my eyes are so dark they look as though someone drew them on. The hair . . . but the hair doesn't matter. It will grow. It seems almost right now, that it should be gone. A penance of sorts. Still, it's as if there's nothing left of me that I recognize. Not the white skin, the dull brown spikes of hair, the twisted mouth.

The eyes should be the same. The shape, the color couldn't change. But the left eyelid hangs heavy, like a broken shade. And the eyes themselves . . . they're like nothing I've ever seen looking out at me from a mirror before. That's what my mother sees, why she talks to me as though I'm a frightened child. That's what my eyes tell her.

"Here." I've seen enough. I hold the mirror out to deBatz.

DeBatz watches me for a long moment. I turn away.

"Give it time," he says. "Things will improve. It isn't as bad as you think it is."

How can he be so sure? I've made this caricature of myself, and I can't even remember what I'm supposed to look like.

Sitting in bed, leaning forward while Basric washes my back, I wonder if this is what they call irony. Funny to remember how furiously embarrassed I once was at the idea of Basric washing me. I look at the limp hand in my lap, and everything I've lost flashes through my mind.

Everything I won't be able to do, from the simplest task like tying my shoes to riding my horse. The thought of Drummer is another gaping hole. I squeeze my eyes closed, but I can't shut thought out for long.

"If Your Royal Highness would now swing his legs over the side of the bed." Basric has been inspired by the physical therapy sessions and applies the principles to every activity. His hands are deft on my ankle. "That's it. Hook the right foot under the left ankle, bracing on the right arm, and now swing."

Just that simple. I don't move. Basric slips my right foot under my left ankle.

"Try, Highness."

I don't want to, but Basric looks as though he might cry. So I try. The left leg inches across the sheet. It's like a hundredweight of stone.

It would be easier to let Basric do this for me. Let him do everything. Why not? Isn't that his job? But what if he wasn't here, or deBatz or Malek or Jiri? What if I had no choice but to learn to do these things for myself? But I do have a choice because of who I am. And it's because of who I am that I've been shot. . . .

Circles. I'm thinking in circles. I jerk my right foot, sliding my left leg over the edge of the mattress so quickly that I tumble over sideways. Basric helps me sit back up.

"Slow and steady, Highness," Basric says in the kind of voice I used to use with Drummer when he was fractious. "It will improve with practice."

I sit still and let him slip a shirt over my arms.

"Would Your Royal Highness care to try the buttons?" he suggests transparently.

Two months ago, he would have wept at the idea of my buttoning my own shirt. Now he wants me to be independent. I shake my head. He sighs and begins buttoning.

The days have taken on a pattern. After Basric's attempts to teach me independent living, we have breakfast. After breakfast, deBatz tries to make me walk.

The last week in the hospital, Kurt—the physical therapist—taught deBatz about the most important techniques to use. To determine the focus of the therapy, he asked what my goal was. It was a familiar question, and I thought I knew the answer. I was fairly certain "going to the bathroom by myself" wasn't what he had in mind. While I was trying to remember, deBatz answered for me.

"To walk again."

That didn't seem like the right answer either, but I didn't argue. Kurt nodded and proceeded to lay out a plan, as though deBatz had asked for directions to the cafeteria.

Now I stand between two steel bars set up in the parlor of the Vrenitzis' house. The bars are only three meters long, but they stretch like an endless corridor in a nightmare. Malek stands on my left (Jiri is on guard) and deBatz kneels behind me and takes my left foot in his hands.

"We want to trigger a feedback mechanism in the muscle by stretching it," Kurt had explained. "The muscle will contract to protect itself from being overstretched and will swing the leg forward. Through repetition, the body and brain will relearn the pattern of movement required to walk."

I feel the muscle stretch across the front of my thigh, into my hip, as deBatz draws my leg backward. From about the middle of my thigh downward, I feel nothing. He releases it, and the leg swings forward.

"Lean into it."

Malek's hands grip my shoulders—the fingers digging in—and push me to the left.

"Come, Highness," deBatz says. "Follow the momentum with the right leg."

But there's nothing to step on. As though I have no foot, no knee, nothing. I feel myself crumbling. Malek catches me under my armpits.

"Try it again," deBatz says, and Malek props me back up on the bars. "Now you know what to expect."

But it's a surprise every time. After half a dozen tries, he gives in.

"It will take time and repetition. The brace you were measured for in the hospital will help. Until it's ready, we will focus on the reflex."

Focus on the reflex. It's a good suggestion. When someone gives me food, I put it in my mouth, chew and swallow. When someone asks me how I am, I say I'm fine. Sometimes the reflex isn't there. When I'm alone, when there's no one to trigger the reflex, I crumble.

At night, a different reflex takes over. I think I'm growing numb to the nightmare, but some nights, it's too much and I wake up screaming. If I could put a face or a name to the crashing red horror, it might help. But as it is, the only face I see is my own.

DeBatz is always there. I don't know when I began to wonder how he got there so quickly. My room is on the ground floor, far from the other bedrooms. The first day Basric helped me into the wheelchair and pushed me into the hall and I saw the cot pushed up against the wall, I almost didn't mention it. I saw it, registered its existence, but didn't have much curiosity about it.

"What's that for?" I asked Basric.

"Count deBatz sleeps there."

I thought he was joking. "Really, Basric. Why is it there?"

I was swamped with shame that deBatz had to sleep by my door so that he could comfort me like an infant. I was determined not to call out again. But I did, and deBatz was there. Calm, never resentful.

I should tell him to sleep in one of the bedrooms, that I'll be all right. But I know he won't listen to me. And deep down, I'm terrified that he might.

I find myself thinking about deBatz, which startles me. Wondering what's changed about our relationship. Is it that I'm basically helpless? Somehow, I think deBatz would have walked away from feelings of pity. What, then?

Because I can't pin down deBatz's reasons, I feel strangely uncomfortable with him. Before, when we stood opposed, it was easy to hate him. Now I'm not sure.

My parents are here. My mother has brought an enormous bunch of flowers that sits in an old crystal vase on the table next to me. Bright yellow and purple, the colors hurt my eyes. Too vivid in the shabby, quiet room. My mother kisses me and steps back, smiling.

"You look wonderful! Your face looks much better, and your hair is growing back in." Her voice and her smile are like the flowers. Too much, too loud. She takes things down a notch. "I hope Stefan isn't working you too hard."

"I'm all right, Mum." Talking is easier, but there's still a slight slur. I wonder if she's right about my face. Since the day we arrived here, I've avoided mirrors.

"We miss you," she says to me.

I miss you, too. That's what I'm supposed to say. But I can't say it. It's not that it isn't true. I feel myself pulled toward them so strongly, I'm surprised the force of it doesn't draw the wheelchair across the space that separates us. But missing them is tied up in too many other things. I feel as though I don't have a right to miss them.

My mother talks on, passing on messages people have asked her to give me. I realize I've been staring at my father's knees, look up and catch him staring back. He looks better than he did in the hospital. At least he's clean-shaven and his hair is combed. But he looks . . . I don't know . . . squashed. He watches me.

DeBatz returns, and with my mother's help, manages to carry the conversation through lunch. It isn't until after they leave that I realize how little my father has said.

"Is something going on in Rovenia?" I ask deBatz.

"What do you mean?"

I shrug and pick at the armrest of my wheelchair. "My father . . . Did you notice? He . . . he seemed very quiet." I shrug again. "I wondered if something was worrying him."

DeBatz leans down to undo the locks on the wheelchair. "I imagine he is worried about you, Highness."

But it's more than that.

"I think you need to rest," deBatz says. "I'll take you to your room."

He helps me sit on the edge of the bed and kneels to untie my shoes. I watch the top of his head. The pale skin in the part of his hair looks strangely vulnerable. Under the skin, only a few centimeters of fragile bone, not enough to stop a bullet.

"I'll wake you in time for supper." He leaves, closing the door behind him.

I close my eyes and see my father watching me. I think deBatz is wrong. It's more specific than concern about me. Something is going on in Rovenia, because of me. Some backlash, and my father is left to clean it up. Two months ago, he would have shouted at me. But not now.

In this alien room with the jungle vines crawling up the walls, longing pierces me. A perverse feeling, always wanting the impossible. Homesickness? For what? A place that would reject me the way I'd rejected it.

I nearly cry out, the sudden loneliness overwhelming. What will happen now? Where will I go if Rovenia doesn't want me? And they don't. I know it, from my father's face. And what will it mean to him? It will mean the end of the monarchy, an end to the thing he loved and was so good at.

Dreams of escape are gone. I'm at the edge of that great black hole, and I want what I've thrown away. A place to belong and people to share it with. And maybe . . . maybe a chance to prove . . . something . . .

34

The next morning the brace arrives, molded plastic and nylon tape and thin metal bars, like a torture device, a piece of machinery I'm supposed to accept as part of me. I don't think it will work. But if it doesn't, I'll sit in this wheelchair for the rest of my life.

DeBatz kneels and fits the brace round my calf. It's complex, taking him nearly ten minutes. I could never manage it on my own. It fits under my foot and extends past my knee, immobilizing my ankle. A pressure-sensitive catch controls the knee joint. It's not heavy. Though I can't feel it against my leg, I had expected the weight to drag. There's an aluminum cane with four little legs and gray rubber grips. It clips over my right elbow and fits into my armpit.

"It's dreadful. I look like Tiny Tim."

"It will not be noticeable under trousers." DeBatz stands. "We can worry about aesthetics later. Let us concentrate on mechanics. Come."

He hauls me to my feet and balances me. The brace clicks when my left leg straightens. I feel a difference, the support my body already recognizes, the weight shifting slightly of its own accord.

"How does it feel?"

I shrug. "All right."

"Keep most of the weight on the right side when you are standing, to keep the catch from unlocking." DeBatz stands on my right, one arm across my back. "Lean to the right and use the momentum to swing the left hip forward. I won't let you fall."

It's not that I don't trust him, but he's asking me to step off a cliff. He's asking me to make my muscles do something my brain can't tell them to do.

"Do you want me to trigger the reflex?"

"No!" Then more quietly, "No."

DeBatz breathes hard through his nose. I recognize the signs of mounting impatience.

"Try. One step," he says. "Or do you prefer the idea of being pushed about in a chair for the rest of your life?"

My hand contracts on the handle. I lean heavily on the cane and fling my body forward. Too much. My leg swings in a circle, the propulsion taking me with it. My body pivots wildly on the point of the cane and I crash to the floor.

"I'm sorry." DeBatz grabs me by the armpits. "I thought I could catch you."

The feeling of falling and not being able to stop myself shakes me.

"Come." He heaves me up. "Let's try again."

I'm shaking so, I can't balance myself. DeBatz holds my shoulders, steadies me.

"Shall I ask Jiri to help?"

"No. I don't want anyone else to see this."

"Very well." DeBatz stands at my left side this time. "Try again."

My left foot comes down, and my knee gives out. Too late I realize I haven't swung hard enough to make the lock catch. I crumple sideways. But deBatz has me round the waist and props me back up, kicking my foot until the brace locks.

"Keep going," he grunts. "The right foot."

"I can't."

Rivulets of sweat run between my shoulder blades, and exhaustion shudders through my muscles. DeBatz straightens me out, arranging my feet. I try again. And again. But I have no control over the swing. And everything hurts. I've got a stitch in my side and the cane feels as though it's about to dislocate my shoulder.

"Again." DeBatz is relentless.

"No."

"One complete step. From the right to the left and back. Then we'll stop."

"I can't. I'm tired."

"Try it with the bars. Or the treadmill."

"No! Let me sit."

"You can't give up," he says.

"I'm not giving up!" I take a breath. "I only want to sit for a minute, all right?"

He helps me to the wheelchair. I sit and shake the cane off my arm. It clatters on the floor. DeBatz sits on the low footstool next to me.

"It will take time. You can't expect the brace to make everything suddenly work."

I turn on him. "I don't!" I lower my voice and look at my knees. "All I know is it's not getting any better. It never will."

"You don't know that. Look how far you've come. Your speech is much better. And you can move your left arm a little. It will come."

"It's too hard. It shouldn't be so hard to simply walk."

"Highness, do you know how fortunate you are? To have Basric and the money to recover here in privacy. And the treatment you received in Budapest. There is nothing like that in Rovenia. You have been in those hospitals. You have seen how bad it is. There are patients there, thousands of them, far worse off than you. What chance do they have?"

I blink furiously. I don't want to hear about how terrible others have it, decent people who don't deserve their lot. . . . Not like me.

"If you were one of them, you probably would not have survived." DeBatz crouches in front of me, his hands on the arms of the wheelchair. "I know it's frustrating, but you must keep trying."

"You don't know. You only want me back on my feet. You don't care how. As long as you can get back to your castle. That's all you wanted, anyway."

His every muscle seems to seize up.

"What do you mean?" His face is so tight, his lips barely move.

"I know why you're doing this," I say to my hands. "You only took this job because they promised to give your family's property back to you."

He straightens and walks across the room, the old *tap-tap-tap* of his stride. I watch his feet coming back, a little faster. He arranges a chair in front of me and sits.

"It's true I did not want this position. My party asked me to accept it. It is also true that the restoration of the Hrad deBatz and the land was an incentive I could not overlook. I am setting up a farming cooperative for the local people. But it is not the real reason—the whole reason I accepted the position."

I look at him. "Why, then?"

"Because I trust my people and want the best for my country. My people chose the monarchy. Rovenia wanted a king and a prince. I was determined to make you the best prince Rovenia ever had. Perhaps it was an unfair comparison, but I wanted to make you into the kind of prince I knew."

He's talking about Ulf.

"Those months in England, I would have liked to strangle you with my bare hands. And these past weeks . . . This hasn't been fun for me, torturing you this way. You think I did it for a run-down old castle? *Bozhk!*" He jams his fingers into his hair.

"I don't know why you did it." My voice is very small.

"Then I'll tell you." He leans forward. "I did it because

I sensed an iron will under that spoiled brat exterior. You remember the fights back in England?"

I nod, my face warm with the memory.

"Every time you fought back, I cheered you because it showed me how strong you were. The kind of man Rovenia needs."

My head jerks up in surprise.

He clears his throat. "I was at fault for expecting you to be like Ulf and resenting you when you weren't. I should have let you be who you are. Now, perhaps, you can be better. I think you can." He smiles. "Don't prove me wrong. I hate to be wrong."

We sit and the silence is full, new ideas falling about me like snowflakes, piling up. DeBatz watches me, his eyes large and brown. Kind eyes. I've never seen them like that. And his kindness is suddenly worse than his earlier antagonism.

I choke, but the words must come out. "Do you think I deserved it?"

"What, Highness?"

"This."

"Oh, Alexei."

There's a buzzing in my head, and I fall forward, against deBatz's chest. He puts his arms round me. Hot tears run down my face and soak his shirt. My shoulders shake.

"Hush. *Dyshka*." He strokes my head. "No one deserves this. No one."

I inhale. A ridiculous, hysterical gulp of air, and mumble into his shirt.

"I didn't mean to be so bad."

"What?"

"All the things I did. The way I acted. I couldn't help it."

DeBatz grasps my shoulders and holds me upright. "What do you mean?"

I'm not sure. I don't really know where the words came from, rushing out with the pathetic tears. I sit up, away from him.

"Do *you* think you deserved this?" he asks.

"No!" As soon as I say it, I know it isn't true. There is a place, in that great hole, where I recognize the rightness of what's happened. "I don't know."

DeBatz makes a noise, a low rumbling of thunder, and sits for a moment, staring at his clasped hands.

"Alexei, you know that I have seen people do terrible things to one another. I saw my best friend murdered in front of me. But I have yet to see anyone do anything they deserve to be killed for."

He reaches out and grabs both of my hands. "Behaving like a spoiled brat is not a crime punishable by death. And in a civilized world, it isn't the right of any one person to take the life of another into their hands. No matter what their reasons."

"Then the person who—who did this, he's said why?"

"Yes." DeBatz stands and picks up the cane from the floor.

"Tell me?" I hadn't meant it to be a question.

He turns the cane in his hand. "I don't think it will help you."

"I want to know."

He sighs and lays the cane across a table. "His name is Jevgeny Biskupic."

So the nightmare has a name.

"He is a former soldier in the national army, discharged after the revolution and unable to find work. He believed the government made a mistake restoring the monarchy, and he was afraid that your behavior made the entire government seem corrupt and would open the way for a Communist overthrow." He turns his steady eyes on me. "He said he had to stop you."

It's surprisingly hard to hear the reasons why someone thought I deserved to die.

"That's what my father said." My voice is rough. "He said I was endangering an entire democratic system. He warned me, but I didn't believe him. I made myself a target."

DeBatz bends down, his hands on the arms of my chair, his face level with mine. "You asked me if there was something bothering your father. Can't you guess? I imagine he blames himself for–" He straightens and makes a vague gesture. "For this. The same as I blame myself, the same as Malek and Jiri and a dozen men and women on the royal parliamentary committee blame themselves. We chose to put you in a position you could not handle. We didn't prepare you well enough. We made mistakes."

"It isn't your fault."

He smiles, half his mouth tilting up. "Fault is often in the eye of the beholder. Nobody deserves what happened to you. No matter what you did, it didn't warrant punishment this harsh."

If I could believe this from anyone, it would be from him. He knows the very worst of me.

"If I don't admit that it's my fault, no one will ever forgive me."

"*Bozhk maj!* From whom do you need absolution?"

Faces flash in my mind. My parents, the staff at the castle, Basric, Sophy, deBatz himself, even Sophy's mother. But the ones that stand out are the blurred faces of all the people who lined up to meet me, waiting hours to shake my hand or hand me flowers. The ordinary Rovenians who looked to me for something . . . something I didn't want them to see. Something I didn't want to see myself. But they can never forgive me.

"Who, Alexei?"

"The Rovenians."

He crouches in front of me again. "Do you think they blame you?"

I shake my head a little. "Don't they?"

He looks at the floor, his hands hanging between his legs, and lets out his breath. "You know how they prayed for you. You have seen the cards and well-wishes they have sent you."

I have. My mother forwards a careful selection to me. They make me feel worse.

"That's different. To pray for someone when they're near death doesn't mean they can forgive me. They hate me. I did my best to make them hate me."

"No. They may not have liked your behavior, but they did not hate you."

He has never lied to me. I'd like to believe him now.

"They chose you. You belong to them. You are part of their history. They will not allow anyone to take that away from them." He smiles. "We are a stubborn people."

Six months ago, his words would have infuriated me. Now? One feeling is swamped by another almost before I can recognize them. Hope goes down to a tremendous wave of remorse so strong it threatens to take me under with it. I'm so sorry. The need to say it out loud is almost overwhelming.

"Do they still want me?" I ask.

His gaze is very level, his eyes unwavering.

"You may have to prove yourself to them."

Is that what I want?

DeBatz stands. "We make mistakes, Alexei. Poor choices. But what is important is that we go forward and try not to make the same bad choices again. To see, to do, to prevail, eh?"

"You called me Alexei." It only now registers.

"You once asked me to call you Alex. Would you prefer that?"

I shake my head. "No. My name is Alexei."

"Very well, Alexei."

"Thank you. . . ."

He holds out his hand. "My friends call me Stefan."

35

"**Please, can we stop?**" I ask, dangling from the harness suspended over the treadmill. After only fifteen minutes, my arms tremble and my shirt is clammy with sweat.

"Why don't we work on the floor, with the cane?" Stefan suggests.

With Malek's help, he unhooks the webbing. I lean against Malek as he helps me off the treadmill and into my chair.

"I'm too tired."

"But we've only started," Stefan says. "Come, Alexei."

"I don't want to!" I rub my forehead. "I'm sorry. I'm tired, and I hate the way I look when I use that thing."

There's a strange tension between us today. So much was said yesterday, and I don't think either of us is ready to talk about it. It needs time.

"Look, can't we take a break? For a little while?"

Stefan sighs. "I'll see if the mail has arrived. We'll try again after lunch."

He leaves and Malek excuses himself to relieve Jiri. I try to rearrange myself more comfortably in the wheelchair. It's an electric one, with a joystick I can control so I can move about fairly easily on my own. Lucky again, depending on how you look at things. I flip the switch and roll across the floor to the desk and stare out the window at the garden, covered in a dusting of new snow. I wonder if it snowed in Rovenia. . . . Jiri crosses the lawn in front of the window, running backward. He scoops up a handful of snow, throws it. I hear Malek shout. Jiri doubles up with laughter.

Stefan comes in with the mail and hands me the packet of cards and letters from my mother. She goes through my mail every day and picks out the things she thinks I ought to see and writes a summary of the rest. "Today you received twenty-six cards and letters of well-wishing from Rovenians, fourteen from Brits . . ." and on down the international roster. Then she says, "Do you remember the visit to the elder hostel? There was a lady there making meat pies. She sent you some cookies, but I didn't think they'd survive the post, so I didn't send them."

Once she told me I'd had a card from Isabelle, which she did not forward. It didn't matter. Isabelle has retreated to where she belongs and where she should have stayed: pure fantasy.

Under my mother's letter are all the cards and letters she thinks I need to see today, all taken out of their envelopes so I can handle them easily. On top is a letter with a sticky note attached to it: "I didn't read this."

It's from Sophy. I had a letter from her in the hospital, but I never answered it. There hadn't been any room, then, to think about her, and I was afraid I'd left it too long and she was out of my life for good. I hold the paper to my face, but it only smells like paper. Embarrassed, I lower it and read.

Dear Alex,

I don't really expect you to answer this. Heck, I don't even know if it will get to you. And I guess you've got a lot of other stuff on your mind right now. I just wanted to let you know I'm back in America, in Pittsburgh with my dad. It's okay, really. The school is okay. Nice to get a decent hamburger again. Ha ha.

There was an article about you in TIME magazine last week. About your whole family, actually. You probably didn't see it. I know you don't like that kind of stuff. But it was good. It was all about how the Rovenian people welcomed the monarchy and how they reacted to your being shot, with pictures of candlelight vigils in all the little towns. It was like someone had tried to take something away from them. Like you're a treasure or something.

Well, anyway, I know you're going to be okay. To see, to do and all that. I've seen it in action, you stubborn griffin, you. You won't let this get in your way. You know, you and the Bat are actually a pretty well-matched pair. I hope you aren't giving him too hard a time. He's the one that really needs the sympathy, not you. I miss you.

Love, Sophy

For a long time, I sit and hold Sophy's letter. I read it over until I can close my eyes and see her soft face and almost hear her voice. And I know that it isn't only that I haven't had time or room to think about her, it's that I haven't let myself. I've missed her too much. More than I could have imagined. It's like reaching for a comforting presence you'd taken for granted and finding it gone.

At the bottom of the letter, Sophy has written her address, her e-mail address and phone number. I boot up the computer on the desk and open the e-mail program. For the first time since the restoration, I have Internet access, mainly so my parents can e-mail me daily. Now I type in Sophy's address and stare at the cursor blinking on the blank page. This isn't the way. It's too cold, too distant.

I look round, but there's no one about. Basric fusses into the room. I can trust him.

"Basric, is there a phone around?"

"Yes, Highness." He crosses the room and comes back with a telephone.

"Thanks," I say absently. I dial Sophy's number.

Basric makes a little coughing sound. "If you don't mind, Highness, may I ask where you are calling?"

I glance up at him. "Pittsburgh."

"I wonder if you remember that there's a considerable time difference between Hungary and Pittsburgh."

"Oh." I hadn't thought of that. But the phone is ringing.

"Hello?" a familiar voice, blurry with sleep, mumbles on the other end.

"Sophy?"

"Who is this?"

I cover the mouthpiece. "Basric, would you mind?" He makes his little bow and leaves. "It's—it's Alexei. Alexei Varenhoff," I say when he's gone.

Silence. "Alex?" A sharp intake of breath, almost a sob. "Oh, Alex! You crazy nut. Do you know what time it is here?"

"I'm sorry. I—I wanted to talk to you."

"No, it's okay. I can't believe it. I'm so glad to hear your voice. You can't imagine—"

She breaks off. Is she laughing or crying? It doesn't matter. Her voice is so familiar, she sounds so close, and I ache to see her again.

"I got your letter today," I say. "I got your other letter too. I'm sorry I didn't answer it. I—"

"Oh God, Alex, don't apologize! I didn't expect you to. I just wanted you to know I was thinking about you."

I close my eyes and see her face in my mind.

"I've missed you. I miss talking to you so much."

She laughs. "Right, I was always so sympathetic and understanding."

"Better than that. You were always real."

"Oh." Silence. "Well, I guess this isn't the moment to tell you my real name is Bootsie von Riebnitz, international spy."

"Bootsie?" I laugh.

She laughs too. "What can I say? I look hot in go-go boots."

More silence. "God, Alex, I was worried about you." She makes a funny choking sound and then laughs, a little hysterically.

"It's okay," I tell her. "I know."

"How are you, really?"

I consider for a moment.

"I'm all right."

We talk a little about rehab. I don't go into the details. She asks about deBatz, my parents, tells me about living with her dad, not seeing her mom since the day she left Rovenia.

Basric sticks his head into the room, coughs politely and says something about lunch.

"I have to go. I'll call you again. Soon." I laugh. "To-morrow."

"You'd better," she says. "Anytime. Even at six in the morning. I'll be here."

"You always were, when I needed you," I tell her. "That meant . . . a lot to me."

"No problem. Take care of yourself, sunlight."

36

In two months, I've learned to stand, keeping my balance for several seconds and regaining it if someone gives me a little push. I can move my left arm a little, though I can't grip with my left hand. I have more control of the left side of my face. But walking is still a challenge. With the brace and the cane, I can make it from one side of the living room to the other, a distance of about fifteen feet. But it isn't pretty. And it's almost completely exhausting. I can't see myself ever doing it where someone other than these men might see me.

No one has said a word about going back to Rovenia, and I'm not ready to think about it. I'm comfortable here, with these men. Even though we hold on to some protocol, I don't feel isolated the way I did at the castle.

When Stefan and I get in a tiff, Malek and Jiri take over the rehab sessions. Malek is firm, steady, making sure I do all my reps. Then Jiri gets out the cards and we play until we hear Stefan coming back downstairs. Malek and Jiri teach me the card games they played in the barracks. Basric cooks the peasant food he grew up with, not the fancy stuff the castle chef made. I've learned to understand their jokes and their references to places and people in Rovenia. They've all seen the worst of me and—they're still here.

It can't go on forever, though. I know that. My parents are more anxious every time they visit, but they can see that my body isn't ready. I don't tell them what's in my mind.

At breakfast, I wait for Stefan to outline the day's tortures.

"I am returning to Rovenia on Friday," he says. "I'll be back in a few days. Malek, Jiri and Basric will look after you while I am gone."

"What for?" I ask. Probably to check on his cooperative farm. I'd forgotten about that. How long has it been now since he's been there?

"I have to report to a parliamentary committee."

"Oh." I look at my plate. "About me." It's not a question.

But he nods anyway and spreads butter on his toast. "Yes."

I suppose they have a right to know what's been going on here. They've been paying for it.

"What will you tell them?"

"I don't know." He gives me that direct, even look. "But there is something I think you have a right to know."

"What?"

"This meeting has been called to determine whether or not—under the circumstances—to continue the monarchy."

"But why? The people voted for the monarchy."

"Things are a bit different now."

I'm a bit different now.

"The restoration hinged on the fact that your father had an heir. There is now, of course, the question of your"—Stefan coughs slightly—"ability to produce an heir."

A hot rush of memory from the hospital, painfully embarrassing sponge baths that proved that vital equipment was in working order. No doubt that was all in the medical report.

"But if you are proved to be incapable of succeeding your father, for whatever reason, if—for example—you are physically incapable, the monarchy will most likely end at the next parliament."

I look down, close my right hand over the still limp left.

"What will you tell them?"

"What would you have me tell them, Alexei?"

"I don't know. Tell them whatever you like."

"I would rather tell them what you like." He puts down his knife. "Now is your chance. You tell me what to say, what to tell them."

Does he know what he's saying? He's holding out the key. I struggle to make sense of a rush of emotions. Relief, fear, anger. Anger that the way out was created by Jevgeny Biskupic. That I've given up half my body for freedom. That no longer being Prince Alexei Varenhoff doesn't look as much like freedom as I thought it would.

"Think about it," Stefan says. "You don't need to decide right now."

But isn't this what I wanted?

"What would it mean—for my father?"

"He would be asked to abdicate. Your parents would be given a pension that would allow them to live wherever they chose."

"Not in Rovenia?"

"No. For a number of reasons, not the least of which is your father's sensibilities, it would not be wise for the royal family to remain in Rovenia."

Is it really down to me? To what I choose?

"What about me?"

"The government will pay for your schooling. You are also entitled to a pension as a former civil servant. As well as a disability pension."

It sounds very final, as though he knows what I'll choose.

"But what would I do?"

"Whatever you like."

Whatever I like?

"What would you have done if the restoration hadn't happened?" he asks.

"I don't know." I struggle to remember. "Just—just live. I really hadn't thought."

I had been sixteen and healthy and anything had seemed possible. That was another time, another person entirely.

"Then just live."

Just live. Go to school, to university, get a job. Never come back to Rovenia.

"But what about the Rovenian people? They voted for the monarchy. Isn't there anyone else? There must be another heir, another line?"

"You know the genealogy. The only other branch of the Varenhoff family ended with Ulf Vrenitzi. You are the last of the Varenhoff line. It ends with you."

The gaping hole is there, waiting. All I have to do is choose. The chance for a life as just Alex, whoever he may be. Or what? A chance to atone? I'm not that noble. If I'm hesitating, it's because I want something. Whatever it is, it's just beyond my reach.

"It sounds as if they've already decided."

"No. But they have been closely following your progress and have made plans for every possible circumstance."

"They don't think I can do it."

"They don't know, Alexei. That is why they must plan ahead."

I close my eyes and the past months, the struggle to stand, to eat, to take one step, crash in my mind. I can't do it. It would be so easy to just say it. Everything is in place. Just live.

"Do you think I can't do it?"

"Do you?"

Is he challenging me? It would be like the old deBatz.

He pushes his chair back and stands. "If you are finished with your breakfast, why don't we try the treadmill again, hmm? You've been making real progress."

Take your time, Stefan told me. And for a day, I let myself imagine what it would be like, to not be Prince Alexei ever again. To not have to worry about every move I make and what people are thinking about me. To never go back to Rovenia.

And then I think of what it would mean for Rovenia. Would it matter that much? To lose this frail connection to the past that I'm supposed to represent? As I am now—damaged—could I be enough to make the sacrifice worthwhile? For all of us? Or would it be better all around if we ended it now, before any more damage is done?

What kind of prince could I be, pushed about in a wheelchair, people staring and feeling sorry for me? No. If I choose to stay—to ask for another chance—I have to do it standing on my own feet, show them I can handle it, that I can serve, that I deserve the chance to try. But I don't know if I'm strong enough. And . . . is Rovenia worth the risk?

I don't know. I can't think here where it's safe and I feel cut off from that life. I go looking for Stefan and find him in the library.

"I want to go with you."

He looks up from the laptop computer on the table in front of him.

"To Rovenia. To speak to the parliamentary committee."

"It isn't really necessary." He touches a few keys and closes the computer. "The trip would be difficult, and I can deliver any message you want to send."

"No. I want to tell them myself. I need to go. It's important."

"I don't think it's a good idea." His eyes pierce me. "If

you return, the people will insist on some sort of celebration. They would line the streets. You are not up to that, and they have not been prepared to—" He stops.

"To see me like this?" I finish for him. "Does anyone have to know I'm there?"

"I don't see how we can avoid it. We have to fly, and that means itineraries and cars and guards at the airports. There is no way to do it secretly."

"We could drive."

"Over three hundred miles? Why is it so important that you speak to the committee?"

"I don't know." I rub my fist against my thigh. "I only know I can't let you do it for me."

He looks at me again, a long look, not that urgent scrutiny. "All right."

I let out my breath. "No one must know. Not even my parents."

"Alexei, you must see them if you return. It would be cruel."

"After the committee. Not before. They mustn't know. You said it was my choice. I don't want them involved in it."

Another long look. "Very well."

The car swoops along the mountain roads, past familiar stands of birch and mountain ash. The fragile green leaves have turned and fallen, covering the spent harebells under snow, protected until spring. We pass a sleigh, the horses shaggy with winter growth. In the distance, the mountains stand out white against a steely sky.

Rovenia in spring had nearly pulled me out of myself and flung me unwillingly into delight, but winter here is almost heart-stoppingly beautiful. It's a world made of lace and bells in the air, the white tops of the mountains holding it all in. I want to open the window and stick my head out and breathe in the icy air, feel the wind on my face. But I'm so tired—worn out by the trip and the rush of emotions—I can only lean back in my seat and let the beauty wash over me.

We've been on the road since before dawn, Malek and Jiri sharing the driving, entertaining each other by singing rude drinking songs. It was strange to step out into the world after so long shut away. In a panic, I almost told Stefan to go without me, that I wasn't ready for anyone to see me. But once on the road, the feeling of movement, the changing scenery were wonderful. I wanted to see everything. I hadn't seen anything beyond the Vrenitzi garden in months. But I fell asleep after a few miles.

Stefan woke me when we crossed the border into Rovenia.

"Look, Alexei. We are home!"

The feeling was overwhelming, an assault. And the fear came as a surprise. It must have shown on my face because when we neared Skejni, Malek took the long way round, avoiding driving through town.

Now my heart pounds in answer to everything we pass. Every part of me recognizes that this is home, not for only a few months a little while ago, but for centuries, down into my bones, written in the very DNA of my cells. This is what I wanted, what I needed, why I had to come back. To find out that I belong here.

"Drive down the alley," Stefan says when we get to Arkady Square. "We'll go in the side entrance."

The car eases down the narrow street that runs between the parliament building and the archives, as it did on the day we came to hear my father speak. I feel numb all over, and I'm not sure whether it's from cold or from ghosts. Malek opens the trunk and unloads my wheelchair. Jiri opens my door and helps me slide into the chair.

"All right?" Stefan asks.

I nod.

Jiri holds the door, gives me the thumbs-up as Stefan pushes my chair into the gloom. The guard admits us and we wait for the lift.

A soft bell sounds and an arrow lights above the door. Stefan pushes me through the open doors into the paneled car and I sit, facing away from the doors. What am I doing? Is Stefan right, am I looking for a sort of absolution? There have been so many emotions, I haven't been thinking clearly. My heart hammers and my mouth goes dry. It's not too late. No one's seen me. I'll tell Stefan to go on and Malek and Jiri can take me back to the car, back to the Vrenitzi house where it's safe.

"Stefan?" But my voice is so low, he doesn't hear me.

The lift stops with a gentle bump and the doors glide open. Stefan pushes my chair into the cool, dim hallway, the wheels humming accompaniment to Stefan's, Malek's and Jiri's footsteps. I've never been in this part of the building. The air of hushed dignity carries through even to this remote hall. A sense of ceremony hangs in the air. Impossible to make what I'm about to do seem insignificant.

The passage is deserted except for a single figure, silhouetted against the light from the large window at the end of the hall. A man, standing, watching us, waiting.

"Who is that?" I whisper over my shoulder.

After a moment, Stefan says, "It is your father."

Anger blots out everything for a second. "You told him."

"No. He is here for the meeting."

"You should have told me." It hadn't occurred to me that he would be part of the meeting. "You won't let him stop me?"

"I don't think he will try."

My father walks down the hall and stops in front of me. His face is tired, lined in a way I don't remember.

"Alexei. What are you doing here?"

"I asked Stefan to bring me."

"He had a right to know, Majesty," Stefan says. "His Royal Highness prefers to speak directly to the committee."

My father's face contracts. "I see," he says. "Give us a moment."

Malek, Jiri and Stefan drift away, and my father kneels beside me. I wait, ready to argue.

"You shouldn't have come here," he says. "It isn't necessary. I want you to go back to the car and have deBatz take you to the castle."

I shake my head. "I came here for a reason."

"I know." He puts his hand on my knee. "But it may be better coming from me. After all, I called this meeting. I'll talk to them."

I stare at his hand, at the gold signet ring with the

entwined *R* and *V,* and it hammers me. He called the meeting. He's the one who thinks I can't handle things anymore. I can't really blame him. Since this whole thing started, all I've shown him is my unwillingness to try. And he thinks that's why I've come, to say I can't do it one more time. But he doesn't know . . .

"Please." It comes out in a hoarse whisper. "Let me do this. I promise you won't be ashamed of me."

"Alexei! I've never been ashamed of you."

I don't think that's true, but it doesn't matter. He takes my head between his hands and looks at me for a long moment. I can just feel the warmth of his palm on the left side of my face. I close my eyes.

Finally, he lets go and stands. "They're waiting," he says over my head.

Stefan comes back and pushes my chair toward a set of heavy oak doors carved with two great rampant griffins.

"Stop," I tell him.

"What is it?"

I'm going to do this right. I bend down and move my left foot off the footrest and flip the rests out of the way. Stefan comes round the chair.

"What are you doing?" he asks.

"Help me up."

He helps me out of the chair and I lean against his shoulder, conserving my strength. Malek comes round, holding my cane.

I shake my head. "I don't want that."

Understanding spreads over my father's face as he stands in front of me.

"Are you sure?" he asks. "Is this what you really want?"

I nod. I've never been more sure of what I want and who I am.

"Do you need my help?" he asks.

"Hold on to my arm."

I point to the chair. "Move that out of the way." Jiri rolls it into the shadows.

Stefan stands at the doors, his hands on the heavy brass knobs. He turns and looks at me and pulls himself up, lifting his chin and filling his chest. Holding my father's arm, I try to imitate him, and he smiles, almost laughs. I close my eyes and think about propulsion and swing-through. I can't rely on the reflex anymore.

"Ready?" my father asks.

"I think so."

"Open the doors, deBatz."

Stefan opens the doors and I step forward.

ROVENIAN WORDS AND PHRASES

ANGLISK (ahn-GLISK) – English

BOZHK MAJ (bozhk mahzh) – my God

DASHKA (DAHSH-kah) – Rovenian monetary unit

DHVU ([d]voo) – an expression of disgust

DLINJIV ZHYD KAVROL ([d]LIN-yiv zheedt kahv-ROLE) –
Long live the king

DO VIDENJA (doe vee-DEHN-yah) – goodbye

DRANYIN (DRAHN-yin) – darling

DYSHKA (DEESH-kah) – quiet

FADIT BURKA (fah-DIT BUR-kah) – traditional pork pie

HORLA BALID (OR-lah bah-LEED) – sore throat (throat hurts)

HRAD (rad) – baronial castle or manor house

JAZHDANYV (yahzh-DAHN-eve) – thirsty

KAVRALYVA (kahv-rah-LEEV-ah) – queen

KAVROL (kahv-ROLE) – king

KAVROLOVICH (kahv-ROLE-oh-VICH) – prince

KYAHK VYJ TSIBAH CHUSTVYIT? (K[ee]ahk veezh see-BAH
SHOOST-veet) – How are you feeling?

KYAHK ZHA VRAM MAHKO PAMATSK? (K[ee]ahk zhah
vrohm mah-KO pah-MAHTSK) – How may I help you?

LUZHTA (LOOSH-tah) – welcome

MAKLA MAZHT (MAH-klah mahzht) – little mother

MANYA ZVOOST (MAHN-yah zvoost) – My name is

NID K'SHORDUV (Need k'shore-DOOV) – Go to hell

NYEN (nyehn) – no

PADMITSA (pahd-MEET-sah) – get up

RHENYI (REHN-yee) – national sport of Rovenia, similar to
    European football (soccer) with elements of rugby

RIVKA (REEV-kah) – river

SPESID TVY UF BAL? (SPEH-seed tvy oof bahl) – Are you in
    pain?

SPETZIVA (speh-[t]ZEE-vah) – thank you

TEVRISH (tehv-REESH) – friend

TVY PA SUKIN-SEN (tvy pah SOO-kin sen) – equivalent to son
    of a bitch

VRESHYNIZ (vreh-ZHEE-neetz) – Highness

YEGRADT ([y]ee-GRAHD[t]) – traditional Rovenian theatrical
    form

ZAHKNIZH (zahk-NEEZH) – shut up

ZHRA (zhrah) – shortened, familiar form of hello

ZHRAFSVYETI (zhrahfs-VYEH-tee) – hello

ABOUT THE AUTHOR

MELISSA WYATT lives with her husband and two sons in York, Pennsylvania, where she was born and raised. Aside from writing and reading, she enjoys old movies, dark chocolate and annoying her family by singing show tunes. She's pretty sure she isn't royalty because her sister used to test her by putting peas under her mattress and she never felt a thing.